"What was so special about last night?"

Kelly's question surprised Jordan. "You ask me that?" he said huskily, his hands firm on her upper arms.

"We *are* married, Jordan," Kelly answered in as light a tone as she could muster. "We're perfectly entitled to last night."

"But you aren't coming back to me?" His eyes were narrowed to icy gray slits.

"I couldn't make a decision like that on the basis of one night together," she shrugged, prevaricating.

"Kelly?" He frowned. "What are you suggesting? That we carry on like this, sleeping together and yet making no commitment to each other?"

She sat back on her heels. Yes, that was exactly what she was suggesting—until he could make her the kind of commitment he could never make before. . . .

CAROLE MORTIMER

is also the author of these

Harlequin Presents

Many of these titles are available at your local bookseller.

For a free catalogue listing all available Harlequin Romances and Harlequin Presents, send your name and address to:

HARLEQUIN READER SERVICE
1440 South Priest Drive, Tempe, AZ 85281
Canadian address: Stratford, Ontario. N5A 6W2

CAROLE MORTIMER

burning obsession

Harlequin Books

TORONTO · LONDON · LOS ANGELES · AMSTERDAM
SYDNEY · HAMBURG · PARIS · STOCKHOLM · ATHENS · TOKYO

For
John and Matthew

Harlequin Presents edition published July 1982
ISBN 0-373-10518-5

CHAPTER ONE

KELLY's face paled and her breathing seemed to stop as she saw the tall arrogant man entering the hotel, the usual blonde on his arm. She would have to be blonde, Jordan had a passion for them. But at least it wasn't Angela Divine. That didn't surprise Kelly either; after five years there would have been a couple of dozen blondes, Angela Divine long ago replaced.

Jordan hadn't seen her as he walked over to the reception desk, so she had ample opportunity to look at him without him being aware of it. He would be thirty-nine now, and he looked it, the grey hair at his temples lending distinction to his bearing, a startling contrast to his jet black hair. The grey hadn't been there five years ago, and the deep lines of cynicism beside his nose and mouth had become all the more noticeable. The grey of his eyes was just as steely, his full mouth set in a firm line, the deep sensuality of his nature held firmly in check.

Kelly stepped back as Jordan and the beautiful blonde got into the lift, and she remained hidden until the lift began to ascend. It had been inevitable that this would happen, that they would meet again sometime, and yet Kelly found she still wasn't ready for it.

Five years ago she had been eighteen, an easy victim to Jordan's lethal charm. She had fallen in love with the leashed vitality of him on sight, and had remained in love with him until the day almost seven months later when her dreams of belonging to Jordan for ever had been destroyed, as surely as the child she had been carrying had been destroyed.

7

She could still vividly remember that day, could remember waking up in that cold clinical room, a sense of doom about her even though she couldn't remember what she was doing there. She had soon found out!

'I'm afraid the baby is gone, Mrs Lord.'

Kelly had blinked up at the young doctor, her mind in a fog. Baby? What baby, she wanted to ask. More to the point, *whose* baby?

'Sleep now, Mrs Lord,' a nurse soothed. 'Sleep now and your husband should be back when you wake up again.'

'Back?' Kelly asked, her mouth very dry. 'Back from where?'

The nurse tucked the bedclothes more firmly around her. 'Mr Lord had to leave, to go to his office, I think.'

'Oh yes,' Kelly accepted bitterly. She had known it would be something to do with his office that would take Jordan away from her when she needed him. She turned away so that the nurse shouldn't see her ready tears. 'Thank you,' she murmured huskily. 'I think I should like to sleep now.'

The nurse looked concerned. 'Would you like something to help you sleep?'

'Why?' Her voice was shrill as she looked up at the other girl. 'I'm not ill, am I?'

'No, of course not. But you must be feeling weak after the baby.'

Kelly frowned, her eyelids starting to droop sleepily without the necessity of drugs. The nurse had mentioned a baby now. She just wished she knew what they were talking about . . .

When she woke again the loss of her baby had shot into her like a knife, the baby she had only carried for five months, the baby who hadn't stood a chance of survival when she had started to miscarry.

Her blue eyes were tightly shut to hold out the cold

reality of daylight for as long as possible. Would Jordan have come back from his office yet, or would he still be putting that first? After all, she wasn't ill, she had just lost the baby that had come to be the most important thing in her life, the baby Jordan had neither wanted or desired.

Her breath caught in a sob and she turned to bury her face in the pillow, crying out her misery and pain.

'Kelly?' A hand caressed her shoulder through the thin material of her nightgown.

She had flinched away from that hand, turning slowly to look at her husband. 'Jordan,' she greeted coldly, her eyes huge and bewildered in her pale face. 'Did you finish your business?' she asked bitterly.

Jordan frowned, a tall man, very attractive, who had stirred many a female heart before their marriage six months earlier, and still continued to do so, as she knew to her cost.

'You were asleep,' his voice was stilted, his manner withdrawn. 'There was nothing I could do.'

'Of course not,' she replied distantly. 'Did you deal with the matter?' She gave a choked laugh. 'Of course you did, what a stupid question.'

'I haven't been to the office, Kelly. I——'

She struggled to sit up, not wanting to listen to him. 'Could you get someone to help me, please?'

He lent over her, his hard presence at once overwhelming her, as it usually did. 'I'll help you,' he sat her forward. 'Just hold on to me while I adjust the back-rest.'

'No!' She shrank away from him. 'Get someone else to help me. Get a nurse. Get anyone but you!' she cried hysterically.

He instantly moved away, his face a shuttered mask. 'There'll be other babies, Kelly,' he said coldly. 'I'm sorry about this one, but——'

'No!' she cried again. 'There won't be any more. I

won't have any more!' She looked at him like a frightened
child, her fingers clenching and unclenching on the
coverlet. 'No more,' she repeated, suddenly all the life
flowing out of her as she collapsed weakly back on to the
pillows.

'You're tired,' Jordan said abruptly. 'Try to sleep now
and I'll come back and see you later.'

'Going back to work, Jordan?' she taunted. 'Or could
Angela be the main attraction?'

Those grey eyes narrowed ominously. 'Angela? You
mean my secretary?'

Kelly's mouth turned back with a sneer. 'If that's what
you choose to call her.'

'You're more tired than you realise,' her husband
snapped. 'You're becoming fanciful. Sleep now and we'll
talk later.'

'I only want to know one thing,' she said coldly. 'When
can I get out of here?'

'A couple of weeks, the doctor said, and even then you'll
still be very weak.'

'I've always been weak where you're concerned,' her
voice was distant, all emotion locked away, 'but not any
more.'

He frowned. 'What are you saying now, Kelly? I realise
you're upset about the baby——'

'What was it?' she asked dully.

Jordan looked startled by the question. 'Don't dwell on
it, Kelly. It's best forgotten.'

Forgotten! She would never forget the loss of the baby,
or the reason behind it. 'What was it, Jordan?'

He gave an impatient sigh at her obstinacy. 'A girl,' he
told her curtly.

'Then perhaps it's as well it died, you wanted a girl
even less than you wanted a boy,' she scorned to hide her
pain.

His hand came out to painfully grasp hers. 'I'd much rather have you alive and well—'

Kelly snatched her hand away. 'Don't spout insincere platitudes to me!' she snapped coldly, turning away from him. 'If you don't mind, I'd like to sleep now.' She snuggled down under the covers in a pretence of sleep.

'Kelly?' he touched her shoulders.

She shook off his hand. 'I'm sleepy. Goodbye, Jordan.'

'I'll see you tomorrow.' There was weary resignation in his voice, but Kelly remained hardened against him.

She waited for the soft click of the door as he left before she allowed the tears to flow. She could still remember it all now, calling at Jordan's office that morning, eager to show him the tiny clothes she had bought for the baby, rushing happily into his outer office to find his secretary's desk empty. She could hear Jordan's even tone as he talked to the girl who had been his secretary for the last year, but it hadn't bothered her that they were working. She had met the other girl a couple of times, and her presence in Jordan's office was immaterial to her.

But the conversation hadn't been! What she had heard that day had shown her all too clearly that Jordan's relationship with his secretary continued outside the office.

She had rushed out of the building as though pursued by the devil. Jordan and his secretary! Oh, she had felt sick, so sick she just ran and ran, not sparing a thought for the baby until she had felt that first searing pain, a pain that was quickly followed by another, and another, until she had thought she would die.

So she had discovered the reason Jordan hadn't been near her since her pregnancy had been confirmed—he had been getting that satisfaction from his beautiful secretary. She had vowed there and then that he would never touch her again, a decision she quickly apprised him of, on returning from the hospital to their home in fact.

'Comfortable?' Jordan tucked the blanket more firmly about her legs.

She nodded distantly. 'Thank you.'

He gave her a long searching look before moving impatiently to get in behind the wheel of the car.

They didn't talk on the drive to their home, as they hadn't talked in the two weeks since she had lost the baby. Kelly had nothing to say to this cold, hard man who was her husband, and he seemed to take his mood from her.

He held her elbow as they entered the house together, refusing to have his fingers dislodged.

'Oh, it's so good to see you, Mrs Lord,' Mrs McLeod, their housekeeper, hurried out into the hallway to greet them.

'Thank you, Mrs McLeod.' She couldn't even raise any warmth for the woman who had shown her nothing but kindness since Kelly's marriage to her employer six months ago.

'Tea in the lounge, I think, Mrs McLeod,' Jordan suggested smoothly. 'I'm sure Mrs Lord would welcome the refreshment.'

'Of course, sir,' the woman smiled. ' I have it all ready. I won't be a moment.'

Once alone Kelly had moved away from her husband and into the spacious lounge that even after six months still managed to convey none of her own personality but was all Jordan. The deep grey velvet curtains either end of the huge room perfectly matched the deep-pile carpet. The black leather armchairs and sofa were just as impersonal, and even the slightly feminine touches of ornaments and clear-cut glass seemed to bring no warmth to the room—as Jordan himself had no warmth.

She couldn't even begin to guess why Jordan had married her in the first place; it certainly hadn't been because he loved her, he didn't know how to love. But love was the reason she had accepted him—her own love for him, a love that had died as her baby had died.

From the moment they had met at a dinner party given by her father, with her acting as his hostess, Jordan had begun to pay her attention. He had asked her out to the theatre that first evening, and for the next month they had met constantly. If Jordan had treated her rather like a child to be humoured she hadn't minded. She had craved only his soul-destroying kisses that had always ended the evening, kisses and caresses that he was always in control of, no matter how she begged for more.

When he had asked her to marry him she had eagerly accepted, her love for him so strong by this time that she wanted only to be with him for all time.

Her father had been less delighted by the news, but despite his mild opposition the wedding had taken place only a month after their first meeting. They had honeymooned in Barbados, with Jordan introducing her to all the sensual delight her body was capable of, seeming to find pleasure in her pleasure, until they both reached the tumultuous climax of their senses.

It was during one of those sun-drenched, love-filled days and nights that Kelly had conceived their child, a child that had seemed the fulfilment of all her dreams. Jordan hadn't shared her enthusiasm, but in her own happiness she hadn't paid this much attention. She had put his reserve down to a reluctance to halt their nights of passion, although she hadn't expected them to come to quite such an abrupt end, the very night she had told Jordan he was to be a father.

'Your father is coming to dinner,' Jordan informed her as they waited for Mrs McLeod to bring in the tea. 'I haven't told him the news. It didn't seem the sort of thing I should tell him over the telephone, even if I'd known where to reach him in the States.'

Kelly's mouth turned back. 'Then I'm going to come as something of a shock to him.'

'Yes,' he agreed tersely, his expression grim.

She patted her flattened stomach bitterly. 'Quite a shock,' she repeated.

'Yes,' he said again, turning to fill a glass with whisky.

Kelly eyed him coldly. 'Isn't it a little early in the day for that?'

Grey eyes raked over her. 'Do you care?'

She shrugged. 'Not particularly.'

His mouth twisted tauntingly. 'I thought not,' he swallowed half the liquid in one gulp. 'What the hell's got into you?' he rasped. 'Losing the baby was traumatic——'

'I'm glad you realise it.' Her voice was harsh.

Jordan gave her an angry look. 'I'm not completely insensitive. But I don't expect this to have changed you out of all recognition.'

Kelly idly picked up one of the cut-glass vases that adorned the alcove, admiring its cool beauty with icy detachment. 'Things like that have a way of making one grow up in a hurry. After all, Jordan, I'm not a child any longer,' she scorned.

'I wouldn't call eighteen old. And I always liked your youthful enthusiasm for everything.'

'Appealed to your jaded senses, did it?' she taunted.

'You see?' he snapped impatiently, swinging her round to face him and knocking the vase out of her hand in the process. It shattered at their feet. 'Oh hell,' he swore, 'now look what you've done!'

'What *I've* done?' she looked at him with accusing eyes, that vase a particular favourite with her. 'You're the one who had to use brute force—as usual,' she sneered. 'Take your hands off me, you—you——'

'Yes?' His narrowed eyes levelled on her mouth.

Kelly could tell he was going to kiss her and she jerked

back, regretting her impulse as she saw the mockery in his eyes. 'Just don't touch me! I hate to be touched.'

'That's not the way I remember it.'

She blushed at his implication, remembering the nights when she had almost begged for his possession of her. Memories of other nights spent in his arms, of his lithe muscular body working a familiar magic on her, made her glare her dislike of him. 'Forget the way you remember it. I don't want——'

'Here we are, then,' Mrs McLeod bustled in with the tea things, beaming happily at the two of them. 'Oh dear,' she spotted the shattered vase, 'did you have an accident?'

'It slipped out of my wife's hands,' Jordan said smoothly.

Kelly compressed her lips to hold back her angry retort. After all, what he said was the truth, but it had only happened because of him. His touching her had been provocation enough for her to drop the vase.

'Never mind,' the housekeeper picked up the pieces. 'It's only glass.'

Kelly could see Jordan's mouth twitch at the understatement. It had been a very valuable vase, one she had been very fond of, and although Jordan didn't share her enthusiasm he could appreciate its value.

She sat down in front of the tea-tray. 'Milk or lemon?' she enquired coldly of her husband.

'Milk,' he drawled slowly. 'There's enough sharpness in this room already.'

Kelly glared at him, conscious of Mrs McLeod still picking up the broken glass. 'Sugar?' she asked with exaggerated politeness.

'No, thanks.' He sat down, his long legs stretched out in front of him. 'But you have some—you need the energy,' he added tauntingly.

She knew he hadn't meant that at all, and her mouth tightened angrily. 'How kind of you to think of my health. Isn't he a considerate husband, Mrs McLeod?'

'Well, of course he is.' The housekeeper finally stood up. 'We've all been very worried about you, Mr Lord most of all.'

'But you had no need to be worrried,' Kelly smiled warmly at the other woman. 'I'm young and resilient.'

'Of course you are. But I was telling Mr Lord he should take you away for a holiday, get you away from here and into the sunshine.'

'No! No.' Kelly studiously erased the sharpness from her voice. 'I—I'd rather not.' She didn't want to go anywhere where she would have to be alone with Jordan.

The mockery in his eyes told her that he knew exactly the reason she had turned down the idea of a holiday. 'Maybe later on,' he said smoothly. 'I can't get away at the moment.'

He couldn't leave his secretary! Angela Divine was beautiful, a tall shapely blonde. She was in her late twenties, ten years Kelly's senior, and Kelly felt sure the other woman would make sure Jordan appreciate her added experience.

Kelly shivered as she remembered what it was like to feel like a woman in Jordan's arms, to know the wonder of his caresses that could quickly turn to demanding passion.

He had been so patient with her on their wedding night, had gradually introduced her to the delights of her own body, until the initial pain of their consummation had seemed as nothing compared to the blinding pleasure that quickly followed.

She pushed these erotic thoughts to the back of her mind as she remembered the day of humiliation that had followed in Jordan's office six months later.

Because of Jordan's inability to get away Kelly had suggested that perhaps she could go away on her own. She had known she had to get away from Jordan; the love she had had for him had turned to hate in such a short time, the love that had seemed to be the pinnacle of her life.

Jordan waited for the housekeeper to leave them before vetoing that idea. 'You aren't going anywhere without me,' he snapped. 'Even if you do have this ridiculous aversion to me at the moment.'

Kelly stood up. 'Go to hell!' she said fiercely, turning in the direction of her bedroom, the bedroom that she had slept in alone since telling Jordan of her pregnancy.

He swung her round before she reached the door, a dangerous glitter in his cold grey eyes. 'Don't ever talk to me like that again, little girl!' he rasped. 'I won't stand for it.'

Tears flooded her huge navy blue eyes. 'And what happens if I do?' she choked. 'I suppose you're going to beat me.' She gave a bitter laugh. 'I suppose you'd like that.'

He shook his head impatiently. 'You ridiculous child,' he chided gently, pulling her against him to bury his face in her thick black hair. 'Cry, Kelly,' he encouraged. 'It will help.'

She at once stiffened in his arm, feeling as cold to human warmth as a beautiful statue. 'I have no intention of crying,' she told him in a stilted voice, shrugging out of his arms with a cool dignity that didn't encourage further contact between them. 'Why should I cry?'

She had cried almost hysterically after losing the baby, and felt as if she had cried herself out. All that was left was a numb feeling—and her hatred of Jordan.

'The doctor told me I have to expect strange moods from you,' Jordan eyed her thoughtfully, 'but don't expect my patience with you to be limitless.'

'I don't expect anything from you,' she said tonelessly.

'Now if you'll excuse me, I'm going to my room to rest before dinner.'

'Our room, Kelly,' he corrected softly.

She gave him a sharp look, dark colour creeping into her pale cheeks. 'I consider it my room, as you haven't chosen to share it with me for several months.'

'I intend changing that now that——'

'Now that I'm no longer pregnant!' she finished shrilly. 'You can do what you choose, but don't expect me to welcome you back.'

'Kelly——'

'I believe I've already said this once today, Jordan, but go to hell!' This time she managed to escape to the bedroom without further interruption.

Once inside she almost collapsed on to the bed, feeling curiously weak. If Jordan was serious about sharing her bed once again then she knew she had to get away from here as soon as possible. Not that she thought he would expect a physical relationship from her just yet, but she couldn't even bear to have him sleeping in the same room as herself.

Why on earth had he married her? In the six months they had been married not one word of love had passed his lips, words of passion and possession, but never love. This had never particularly bothered her, their love-making seeming to show her the depth of his feeling for her, and yet even that hadn't been hers alone; she had been sharing him with his sexy secretary, and heaven knew how many other women.

She had fallen asleep soon after going to her bedroom, woken up to find there was only half an hour left before her father arrived. As she swung her legs to the floor Jordan came in from the adjoining bathroom, dressed only in a navy blue towelling robe, Kelly instantly stiffened at the intimacy of the situation, although the cool look she gave him showed him none of her tumultuous feelings inside.

'You should have woken me,' she remarked distantly.

'Should I?' he drawled, rubbing his damp hair dry with a towel. 'You said you wanted to rest.'

'But not for this long.' She pushed her hair back, forcing herself not to be aware of the way Jordan's towelling robe had fallen open at the chest to reveal his smooth dark skin and the silky mat of dark hair that grew there. 'You'll have to entertain Daddy while I shower and dress.' She turned away.

Jordan threw the towel on the huge double bed they were to share from now on, moving towards her with a determination she knew of old. 'Entertaining your father wasn't quite what I had in mind for my immediate future,' he murmured, his eyes on her mouth. 'Come here,' he ordered huskily.

'Not just now.' She stood up to begin looking through her numerous evening dresses in the floor-to-ceiling wardrobe, dresses she hadn't been able to wear the last few months with the thickening of her waistline. Looking down at her slenderness, it had seemed hard to think that she had ever been carrying Jordan's child.

'Kelly!' his hands came down on her hips, pulling her back against him. 'God, I've missed you in my arms,' he groaned into her throat.

Kelly felt sick, his touch almost obscene to her. 'Please, Jordan,' she squirmed away from him. 'This is hardly the time for that sort of thing.'

'That sort of thing?' he repeated softly. 'All I wanted to do was kiss my wife, maybe hold her against me for a while.'

She gave him a vague smile. 'We don't have the time for that, Daddy will be here soon, and neither of us is ready to go down and greet him.'

'Damn Daddy,' he said viciously, his face darkening angrily. 'You don't want me to kiss you, is that it?'

She had shuddered at the very thought. As far as she knew he could even have been with Angela Divine while she was in hospital, and now he wanted to kiss her! 'That's right,' she agreed unhesitantly. 'I have no desire to be kissed by you.'

'That's what I thought.' He turned away.

She had felt nothing in his arms, nothing but a cold emptiness that bore no resemblance to her former love for him. She felt nothing but hate for him, felt none of the love, and none of the pleasure of just being with him. She had known in that moment that their marriage had to end.

Kelly shuddered back to an awareness of her surroundings, sure that only minutes had passed since she had seen Jordan step into that lift, and yet in that time she had relived all the pain and disillusionment she had suffered at his hands.

To him their marriage vows had meant she became his exclusive property, while he still continued to live and act like a bachelor. He must have thought her so naïve, must have found her childish pleasure in being his wife so amusing.

Well, she was a woman now, five years older—and wiser, she hoped. She was a calm self-assured woman who was unnerved by little. She lived with her father, played his hostess, and had heard nothing from her ex-husband since the evening she had walked out on him. Not that he actually was her *ex*-husband, there had been no divorce. But although she had retained his name she had considered herself a free woman for the last five years. And Jordan had assuredly considered himself a single man!

Her father had been her strength from that first night,

in the end accepting her pleas for him to let her go home with him. It had all been so much easier than she had thought it would be, as her fears of Jordan coming after her had never materialised. For all his threats that she would never be allowed to leave him she had been calmly allowed to walk out of his life for ever.

And now he was here, in the same hotel as she was.

She would have to book out of here as soon as possible. She hurried over to the reception desk, aware that once again she would be running away from Jordan, but also knowing that with him here it was the safest course. How he would love a situation like this, would find her embarrassment amusing.

She smiled at the beautiful girl behind the reception desk, subconsciously wondering whether Jordan had found the young girl attractive. Jordan had a passion for blondes, which made it all the more surprising that he had chosen to marry her. She had had long black hair when he had last known her, although it had now been styled into a becoming bob, framing the thinness of her pale face, emphasising the intensity of her navy blue eyes.

She had been a step out of character for Jordan, a deviation from the usual type of woman he was attracted to. But that he had been deeply attracted had been obvious from the first, and once they had been married not a day went by when she didn't know the deep fierceness of his possession. Until she had told him about the baby! Knowing she was carrying his child had turned him off her physically, and with the added strain of this estrangement from her husband's arms she had been forced to acknowledge they had little else to keep them together.

'Mrs Lord?' The beautiful curvaceous blonde behind the desk smiled at her enquiringly.

Yes, she decided, Jordan would like this girl. She was just his type, tall, with long shapely legs, her figure on the

fuller side rather than slender. Jordan must have had a
brainstorm when he married her, Kelly thought bitterly.
She was very slender, boyishly so in recent years, and she
wasn't an inch over five feet tall. A little bundle of dyna-
mite, her father jokingly called her.

Her father! God, she had been so wrapped up in her
thoughts of Jordan that she had completely forgotten the
worry over her father. The two of them had been involved
in a car accident four days ago, and while she had been
uninjured, her father had been in a coma ever since. She
had in fact just been on her way back to the hospital
when she had seen Jordan arriving at the hotel.

'If you're looking for your husband, Mrs Lord,' the
receptionist spoke again, 'he's already gone up to your
suite.'

That shook Kelly out of her wandering thoughts. 'He's
gone *where?*' she asked disbelievingly.

'He just went up to your suite, Mrs Lord,' the girl
repeated, frowning her puzzlement.

Kelly's mouth set mutinously. 'Thank you,' she said
tightly, turning away.

So Jordan knew she was here. He was even now in *her*
suite. Well, they would see about that!

There was no evidence of him when she let herself into
the suite of rooms she had been occupying the last few
days, everywhere in silence. Perhaps the girl on the desk
had got it wrong. Before she could investigate any further
there came a quiet knock on the outer door.

'Mrs Lord,' the young manager stood outside, 'I just
came to check that you have everything you need.'

Kelly frowned. On the brief occasions she had been
back to the hotel, this man had been courteous enough,
but he had certainly never bothered to make this sort of
effort as regards her welfare before. 'Everything, thank
you. Although my husband———'

'Ah yes,' the manager acknowledged eagerly. 'Does Mr Lord have everything he wants too?'

'Yes, thanks, John,' answered a deeply masculine voice from behind them, a voice that was unmistakable to Kelly. 'I have everything I want,' he added, 'or need.'

Kelly had swung round with a gasp at the first sound of that voice. Jordan stood in the bedroom doorway, fortunately not in the bedroom she had put her things in!—and he was dressed only in a white towelling robe, his damp hair evidence of the fact that he must have been taking a shower when she had presumed he wasn't really here.

'Jordan . . .' she breathed his name weakly.

He didn't look at her, smiling at the manager. 'Thanks for your concern, John. If we find we need anything we'll give you a call.' When the younger man had left Jordan finally turned icy grey eyes on Kelly, his gaze narrowing as he took in the tailored dark grey suit and crisp black blouse she wore, her hair short and gleaming, her make-up light, her huge bewildered eyes the only splash of colour in her pale face. 'Kelly,' he greeted curtly. 'What the hell have you done to yourself?' His look was scathing now. 'You look a bloody mess!'

CHAPTER TWO

Her temper sparked into life. 'After five years is that all you have to say?'

He shrugged, strolling back into the bedroom. 'It happens to be the truth.'

Kelly followed him. 'How do you expect me to look?' she snapped her resentment. 'My father is lying dangerously ill in hospital, I'm hardly likely to look full of the joys of spring.'

Jordan took brown trousers and a clean cream shirt out of the wardrobe, pausing to towel dry his hair. 'I didn't mean you look a mess, I meant the *way* you look is a mess.'

She flushed. 'What do you mean by that?'

He threw the towel down on the bed, looking at her consideringly. 'You're twenty-three and dress like a woman ten years older. Where on earth did get those prudish clothes? You look as if you're on your way to a funeral,' he added dismissively.

The cruelty of his words cut into her like a knife. 'My father is ill, I would hardly wear a flaming red dress,' she choked.

'Why not?' He untied his robe, smiling as she hastily turned away. 'I'm no different to look at than I was five years ago,' he taunted. 'And you used to like looking at my body then—you used to like touching it too.' He chuckled at the anger she couldn't hide. 'And why can't you wear a flaming red dress? I'm sure it would cheer your father up more than that outfit.' He made no effort to hide his derision for her smart suit and blouse.

'My father can't see my "outfit" at the moment,' she informed him bitterly. 'He's unconscious, and has been since the accident happened.'

Jordan nodded, pulling on the dark brown trousers and cream shirt, leaving several buttons undone on the latter, revealing the thick mat of hair on his chest, this too liberally sprinkled with grey. 'I ascertained that much from the doctor.'

Kelly's eyes widened. 'You've been in touch with the hospital?'

He gave her a derisive look. 'Obviously,' he said dryly. 'And?'

Jordan raised his eyebrows. 'And I don't suppose they told me any more than they told you.'

'What *did* they tell you?' she asked desperately.

He shrugged. 'Not a lot. Although the coma is apparently lightening.'

'It is?' Kelly said eagerly, watching as he pulled on the jacket that matched his trousers, the material fitting tautly across his broad shoulders.

He brushed the damp thickness of his hair back from his face, the style impeccable, as was the rest of his appearance. 'So they said,' he nodded.

'Then I must get back to the hospital. I only came back to wash and change.'

'So I gathered.' Jordan gave her a searching look. 'You've been sitting with him day and night since the hospital discharged you—and I must say you look as if you have.'

'Will you stop insulting me!' To her shame tears flooded her eyes, their colour even a deeper navy than usual. 'I— I can't take it at the moment!' The tears started to fall, and she began to sob, unable to stop crying once she began.

She felt Jordan take her into his arms. 'This is long

overdue,' he muttered gruffly.

Kelly stiffened the instant he touched her, trying to break out of his embrace, finding that she wasn't as immune to him as she had thought herself to be the last five years. Whenever she had thought about Jordan during that time, which even though she hated to admit it, had been often, it had always been with the numb removed feeling, with the memory of what he had done to her and their unborn child.

But now he wasn't removed at all, and the quicksilver excitement that coursed through her body made her struggles for release all the more fierce. 'Take your hands off me!' she ordered in a chilling voice. 'Before I scream the place down,' she threatened.

He stepped back, his hands held defensively in the air. 'Never let it be said that I held a woman against her will.'

'Is that why you let me go so easily five years ago?' Kelly said bitterly.

Jordan's air of taunting left him, his face taking on an expression of hauteur. 'You wanted to go.'

'Yes, I did. And I've never regretted it,' she spat the words at him. 'Never!'

'Not even once?' he scorned, his grey eyes blazing. 'Are you telling me that you've never lain in your bed at night and wished for me to be at your side? That you've never longed for the perfect lovemaking we always had?'

Had she longed for those things? Not consciously! But subconsciously? Oh, *yes*, she had wanted him, had ached for him as an addict must long for his particular brand of addiction. But until this moment these longings had never been allowed free rein, any of the more intimate memories of their relationship put firmly to the back of her mind. And yet fifteen minutes ago, at the first sight of Jordan

after five years, she had relived every moment of their
time together as man and wife.

Their lovemaking had been perfect, without inhibitions,
each partner desiring to give the other the extreme in
pleasure. And for all of her initial inexperience Kelly *had*
given Jordan pleasure, had excited him until he lost all
control. At the time he had told her she was the only
woman to affect him that deeply, and knowing of the
tight control he had over the rest of his life, she could
believe him. But even that hadn't been enough for him,
she hadn't been enough for him, he had still needed his
other women.

'What did you mean just now about my crying being
long overdue?' She didn't answer his intimate questions,
pulling a shield over the erotic pictures they had conjured
up from the past.

'As far as I know, you've never cried for the loss of our
child.'

Kelly paled when seconds ago she had been blushing.
'Never cried . . .!' she choked. 'My God, I cried, I cried
until there was nothing left.'

'And when you'd finished crying?' His eyes were
narrowed. 'Why didn't you come back?'

'Come back?' she frowned. 'To you?' she scorned.

Jordan stiffened, his expression darkening. 'I'm your
husband.'

'Oh yes?' she taunted. 'And what do you call the
beautiful blonde who arrived with you just now?'

'Janet? She's my personal secretary.'

'How original!' Kelly drawled, picking up her handbag. 'Well, if you'll excuse me, I'm going to the
hospital.'

'What a coincidence, so am I.' He moved to open the
door for her.

'*You* are?' she gasped. 'But why?'

Jordan gave her a look of open disgust. 'I'm going to see my father-in-law. A natural courtesy, I would have thought.'

Kelly allowed him to take her elbow and guide her out of the hotel and into the waiting limousine. 'I wouldn't have thought that relationship counted,' she said stubbornly.

Jordan relaxed back against the cream leather upholstery, his hair even darker against the light colour. 'Maybe it doesn't,' he lit a cheroot with lazy enjoyment, the familiar aroma soon filling the car. They were a special blend, made exclusively for Jordan, and Kelly found she had missed their smell.

Jordan had always liked to smoke one of these cheroots after they had made love, when they would relax in bed together, and Jordan would tell her about his day. Then they would make love again before dozing off into a contented sleep.

'Your father is still a friend of mine,' he continued. 'And was long before I met and married you.'

'Yes,' she acknowledged jerkily. 'I'd forgotten. I'm sorry.'

He gave a haughty inclination of his head. 'I realise you're distressed,' he accepted. 'How did the accident happen?'

Kelly swallowed hard, instantly reliving that split-second crunch of metal upon metal, the front of their Rolls-Royce almost caved in completely on her father's side. The young couple in the other car had been unhurt, Kelly had received only cuts and bruises, and her father had been unconscious ever since.

She shrugged now. 'It was just one of those things, no one's fault.'

'And you?' Jordan looked at her closely. 'You weren't hurt?'

'No.'

'The hospital told me you were admitted for two days.'

Her eyes flashed. 'They had no right——'

'They had every right, damn you!' He stubbed out the half-smoked cheroot with savage movements. 'I have the right to know about the health of my wife!'

Kelly sat stiffly at him side. 'How did you know about the accident?'

'I was in the States on business, and a friend of mine wired me the news.'

'A friend?' she probed.

Jordan gave a humourless smile. 'I do have one or two, you know.'

'Yes, I do know,' she said tightly. 'I just wondered if I knew them too.'

'Ian Smythe,' he supplied tersely.

'Ian!' Her face lit up with pleasure. 'Does he still work for you?' Ian had been Jordan's personal assistant five years ago, and Kelly had always liked him.

Jordan scowled. 'No. He works for himself.'

'He does?' she asked interestedly.

'Mm.' Jordan's mouth twisted with derision. ' He very sensibly married Anthony Miles' only daughter.'

Anthony Miles had been a big industrialist, very rich, who had died suddenly of a heart attack just over a year ago. 'Ian is married to Laura Miles?' Kelly asked dazedly.

He nodded. 'He has been for a few years now.'

'Then I'm sure it wasn't "sensibly" done at all,' she defended indignantly. 'Ian wouldn't marry for any other reason than that he was in love.'

'Love!' Jordan scorned. 'Laura is attractive enough, in a sweet way, but I wouldn't want her for my wife.'

'But then she isn't, is she?'

'Thank God!'

'Are they happy together?'

He shrugged. 'They seem to be.'

'Then that's all that matters.'

'Not really,' he drawled. 'We *seemed* to be happy, but you still walked out on me.'

'And you know why,' Kelly said tightly.

'It was my child too! But you didn't see me walking out on my responsibilities——'

'Responsibilities!' she cut in shrilly. 'You call our child a *responsibility*?' she demanded angrily.

'In a way——'

'What way?' Kelly was furiously angry. 'Because you didn't want it? Because it was a nuisance to you? Because——'

'Shut up!' he ordered through gritted teeth. 'Shut up if you value your life.'

There was such a dangerous glitter in his eyes that Kelly instantly went quiet. Dry sobs racked her body. Jordan had just told her more than adequately his true opinion of the baby she had loved so much, and she hated him anew for his cruelty.

'I'm sorry,' he finally said in a calmer voice. 'We never were able to converse reasonably about the subject. They found nothing wrong with you after the accident?' he returned to their conversation of a few minutes ago.

'I was only in for observation, just a standard thing.'

He dismissed the chauffeur when they reached the hospital, and Kelly felt very small and vulnerable next to Jordan as he guided her to her father's room. She had forgotten how protected she had always felt with him, how fragile he had always made her feel. And after the last few days of trauma it was nice to let him take charge, to lean on him a little.

Her father lay pale against the pillows, a sterile white

dressing on his forehead, the thin tube in his arm feeding him the necessary fluid for his body.

'He looks better than he did,' Kelly told Jordan. 'He did have electrodes on his chest attached to this huge machine, and instead of that little dressing on his temple he had a huge bandage around his head.' She shivered as she remembered her first sight of him after the accident. 'I thought he was dying,' she revealed huskily.

'The doctor told me that they're hopeful of a complete recovery,' Jordan told her gently.

'They told me that too.' She sat down in her usual chair beside her father, taking his hand into her own. 'I usually talk to him for a while. I know it sounds silly, but I think it helps.'

'I'm sure it does.' Jordan stood at the foot of the bed. 'You go right ahead, I'm going to see if I can talk to the doctor.'

Kelly hardly noticed his departure, her attention all on her father. She had first started talking to him hoping that the sound of her voice would jog something in his memory, break this deadlock. She talked about everything and nothing. So far there hadn't even been the flicker of an eyelid, but the doctor had told her constant talking on her part certainly couldn't do her father any harm, and it could do him a lot of good.

Today she had something new to talk about. She told him of Jordan's arrival here, of how he had unexpectedly booked into her hotel. That was another thing she had to ask Jordan about, what he had been doing in *her* suite. She had been too angry to think of asking him that earlier.

'No change,' Jordan reported when he came back. 'He's slowly coming out of it, but it could take a few more days.' He pulled up a chair and sat beside her.

Kelly nodded. 'Thank you. Jordan, earlier, at the hotel, what were you doing in my suite?'

'*Our* suite,' he corrected unhurriedly.

She gave him a sharp look. 'What's that supposed to mean?'

'It means, my dear Kelly, that you are in fact staying in my suite. When you booked in as my wife you were automatically put in the suite I rent all year round.'

She gasped. 'I'm in *your* suite?'

'Correct,' his mouth twisted tauntingly. 'You don't like that, do you?'

'No,' she agreed tightly. 'I had no idea . . . I'll get another suite when I get back.'

Jordan's eyes became palely grey. 'You'll do no such thing.'

'I——'

'You'll stay put, Kelly,' he told her grimly. 'How do you think it will look if I'm in one suite and my wife is in another?'

'Since I'm your *estranged* wife I would have thought it would look perfectly normal.'

'You'll stay put,' Jordan repeated tautly.

'No——'

'Yes! Don't be so damned ridiculous. I'm not about to claim my conjugal rights, so you have no need to worry on that score. Besides, we'll rarely be there at the same time.'

'We won't?' Her cheeks were still flaming from his reference to 'conjugal' rights.

'No. The doctor thinks that your method of talking to your father is what's helping him. So I propose we take it in turns to sit and talk to him.'

'You have no need to do that, Jordan.' She looked down at her father. 'I realise how busy you must be, how im-

portant your work is to you. There's no reason for you
to——' she broke off as he roughly grasped her chin, forcing her to turn and look at him.

'There's a damned good reason,' he snapped angrily.
'You!'

'Me?' Her eyes widened.

'Have you taken a good look at yourself lately?' His
gaze ran slowly over the gauntness of her body. 'I bet in
denims and a shirt it's hard to tell what bloody sex you
are!'

Kelly put up a selfconscious hand to her hair. 'I know
I've lost weight——'

'Lost weight!' he scorned. 'You're skeletal! Look at you,
girl, you're all eyes.'

She blinked back the tears. 'I haven't felt like eating
the last few days.'

His hand left her chin to rest lightly on the side of
her father's bed, drawing attention to the lean strength
of his fingers, the fine mat of hair on the back of his
hand and wrist. 'This has been going on a damned sight
longer than the four days your father has been ill. And
you never used to be tearful like this either. That's the
third time in a matter of minutes that you've started to
cry.'

'I'm sorry,' she sniffed inelegantly.

'Don't be—it's a damn sight healthier than the ice you
were encased in the last time I saw you.'

Kelly's hold on her father's hand tightened. She was so
defenceless without her father's support, making her
realise how much she had come to depend on him since
leaving Jordan. She would, in all probability, never
have left Jordan if it hadn't been for her father's
strength, would have stayed with Jordan knowing of his
other women. Her father hadn't liked the fact that she
had wanted to leave Jordan, had begged her to re-

consider, but in the end had accepted her decision. He had never asked for her reasons, and she had never volunteered them.

'I wasn't encased in ice, I'd just come to my senses, emerged from the stupid dream I'd had of us living happily ever after. How childish you must have found me, Jordan,' she added lightly.

His expression was bleak. 'I found you—enchanting. You were like a breath of fresh spring air after having been in a smoke-filled room.'

'You mean I was naïve,' she scorned dryly.

His grey-eyed gaze ripped into her. 'I mean you were enchanting,' he repeated tautly.

She drew a ragged breath. 'Well, I'm sure you've met plenty of other women you've found just as—enchanting. Janet, for instance.'

'Janet is my secretary, nothing more.'

'Maybe you just don't think of it that way, maybe you just consider sleeping with your secretary as part of her usual duties,' she said with remembered bitterness. 'I suppose it's easier if it's all treated in a businesslike manner.'

'You suppose what's easier?' Jordan bit out.

'You know very well what I mean. How many—secretaries have you had since we parted?'

He was frowning darkly. 'What are you implying?'

'How many, Jordan?'

'I've had three secretaries——'

'Only three?' she taunted. 'You do surprise me.'

'Kelly!' he warned angrily.

'Were they all blondes?'

Jordan frowned. 'Blondes?'

'Well, you're one of those men who prefer blondes.'

'Then why did I marry you?' He looked pointedly at her black hair.

'I've thought of that myself, and I think you must have just had a temporary lapse. Anyway, that's all past history,' she dismissed curtly. 'Do you want to stay here now or do you want me to?'

'We were in the middle of a conversation,' he told her grimly. 'Neither of us is going anywhere until it's finished.'

'As far as I'm concerned we were finished years ago. Now are you going or staying?'

'I'm staying.'

Kelly stood up. 'Then I'm going.' She bent to kiss her father gently on the cheek.

Jordan stood up too. 'Don't think this conversation is over, it's far from that, but we'll continue it at a more—convenient time.' His last words were in the form of a warning.

Her head went back challengingly. 'I'll look forward to it. I'll be back in a couple of hours.'

'Kelly . . .' he stopped her as she reached the door.

'Yes?' She turned to look at him, her breath catching in her throat at his blatant masculinity, the sexual magnetism he emitted without any visible effort on his part. He was thirty-nine now, and Kelly didn't doubt that he would still be lean and attractive in twenty or thirty years' time.

'Didn't you forget something?' he asked softly.

She looked down at her handbag, the only thing she had brought with her. 'No, I don't think so,' she frowned.

'I happen to think that you did.' He came slowly towards her, a look of determination in his face.

Kelly started to back away, not liking that look at all. There was a definite air of threat about him. 'Wh-what do you want?'

'What do you think?' he drawled, reaching out and pulling her slowly into his arms.

'No . . .' she had time to cry before his mouth claimed hers.

It was as if she were fainting, everything starting to spin, the only reality Jordan and the firm strength of his body. He crushed her to him, every bone in her body seeming to snap with the fierceness of him. His mouth ravaged hers into submission, kissing her like a man in a desert must grasp at a glass of sparklingly clear water.

Kelly's hands clung to his shoulders, her body bent like a reed to the hard demand of his. It was like she remembered it being, the mad excitement that made her quiver, the inability to do anything other than kiss him back, standing on tiptoe to more than meet the response he demanded.

Suddenly his mouth gentled on hers, tasting her lips as if they were nectar, holding her head immobile by his hands in the silky softness of her hair, finding the sensitive nerve in her nape, groaning his satisfaction as she trembled against him. Jordan knew her body better than she knew it herself, knew everything that gave her pleasure—and he hadn't forgotten a single thing!

Kelly's sensibility returned to her with effort, and she wrenched away from him, breathing heavily as she gazed up at him with wide apprehensive eyes.

His hair was ruffled, a slight flush to his hard cheeks. 'You'll have to get some more meat on you before I do that again,' he drawled, straightening his tie. 'It's like holding a sack of bones in my arms.'

Her eyes burned with a fierce anger. 'Then don't hold me! I would prefer for you never to touch me again.'

'Can't be done, I'm afraid,' Jordan told her calmly. 'You see, I like touching you, kissing you, I always did.'

'Me, and a hundred other women!'

His mouth twisted. 'There don't happen to be a hundred other women here at the moment.'

'Then wait until you get back to the hotel and pay Janet a visit!' She closed the door decisively behind her as she left.

'Ah, Mrs Lord,' the young Sister who had been helping with the care of Kelly's father smiled at her as they met in the corridor. 'Your father is improving all the time.'

'Yes,' Kelly gave a jerky smile. 'Jordan—my husband is with him now.'

'Ah yes,' the smile the other woman gave indicated that she had already met Jordan—and liked what she had seen. 'You must be relieved that you were at last able to contact him so that he could come home and be with you.'

So that was the story Jordan had given them! 'Yes.' There was no point in disputing what he had told them.

'He's in with your father now, you said?'

'Yes,' Kelly confirmed.

'I'll take him in a cup of tea, shall I?'

'He would like that. Thank you.' Kelly gave a tight smile. Yes, Jordan would like that very much. This young Sister, Sister A. Fellows it said on her plastic name-plate, was a honey-blonde, and her uniform showed what a perfect figure she had, her legs long and shapely. Just Jordan's type. It seemed to be that wherever she went there were women who were just his type!

Sister Fellows patted the smooth style of her hair. 'I'll see to it now. Perhaps I'll see you later, Mrs Lord.'

But Kelly could tell the other woman was already thinking of her next meeting with Jordan. 'Perhaps,' she agreed tightly, walking away with hurried steps.

She had plenty of time to think when she got back to the hotel, plenty of time to think of the way Jordan had just kissed her. To say she had been surprised by the move was putting it mildly, it had been absolutely the last thing she had expected to happen.

Remembering the way she wouldn't even let him touch her after losing the baby, she found it all the harder to accept that she had gone into his arms just now as if it hadn't been five years since it had last happened.

She could still remember the last kiss Jordan had given her, his anger and utter frustration. Her father had duly arrived for dinner the night she had got home from hospital, and his shock on seeing her had been quite understandable.

'It's terrible, terrible,' he kept muttering, obviously deeply upset.

'Yes,' Jordan had finally put a stop to this, 'but there'll be other babies, in time.'

'No!' Kelly cried. 'No more. Not ever.'

'The doctor said there was no reason why you shouldn't be able to have another baby in a year or so.'

'Damn what the doctor said!' she said shrilly. 'I meant *I* don't want any more.'

'Of course you do,' Jordan chided, doing his best to keep his temper with her. 'You've always wanted children.'

'Not yours,' she spat at him. 'I don't want any more children by you!'

'Kelly——'

'Keep out of this, David,' Jordan ordered tautly. 'This is between my wife and myself.' His narrowed eyes fixed on Kelly. 'Are you saying you don't want to sleep with me any more?'

'Jordan, I don't think——'

'Stay out of this, David!' he was told fiercely. 'If you don't like the conversation then go and wait for us in the lounge.'

'Yes, do that, Daddy.' Kelly's defiant gaze hadn't left Jordan, the naked fury in his face.

'Jordan——'

'Just leave us for a while, David,' Jordan had told him, and with extreme reluctance he had finally done so. 'Now,' Jordan once more turned to her, 'just say what you have to say and let's have this out in the open.'

'I'm leaving you,' she told him calmly. 'Tonight. Right now. I'm going home with my father.'

'And you think I'll let you do that?'

'I know you can't stop me,' she said coldly.

'Like hell I can't!' His chair went back with a clatter as he stood up from the dining-room table, pulling her to her feet too. 'There's always been one way I can reach you.' His mouth came ruthlessly down on hers.

Kelly had stoood like ice as he devoured her with a restless hunger, trying his damnedest to evoke a response in her. But she hadn't given him one, had been revolted by his touch as she thought of him kissing Angela Divine in exactly the same way.

Finally he pulled back, thrusting her away from him with a moan of self-disgust. 'So you can't even kiss me now,' he sneered. 'Okay, go with your father, and when you come to your senses give me a call. I'll come and bring you back to me, where you belong.'

'I belong to no one,' she snapped icily. 'Especially you. I hate you!'

'And God knows that at this moment I hate you too!' Jordan slammed out of the room, and seconds later out of the house too, the silence deafening after his departure.

Her father had tried to persuade her to leave it for a few days, to give herself time, but she had refused, packing a suitcase and leaving with him before Jordan returned.

Maybe Jordan's question this afternoon about why she had never gone back to him had been referring to that scene. He had left the door open for her it she ever wanted to go to him. But she hadn't even thought about it, had travelled with her father on business, had been his hostess in his Hampshire home. Going back to Jordan had never occurred to her.

Then why had it occurred to her now?

Kelly was sitting with her father when he woke up late the next afternoon. She had been talking to him as usual, had been telling him of her confusion about Jordan.

Jordan had been right, they saw little of each other, and when they did meet he was always coolly polite, almost as if that incident in this very room had never happened.

It was as she was telling her father this that his eyelids had begun to flicker, his lips to move slightly. When his eyelids suddenly opened Kelly almost burst into hysterical sobs, pressing the button by the bed to bring the doctor to the room.

She stood up, smiling down tremulously at her father. 'Daddy?' she said huskily, her tears choking in her throat. 'Daddy, it's Kelly.'

'Hello, darling,' he spoke as if he hadn't been unconscious for the last five days, as if he had just woken up from an afternoon nap. 'What time is it?'

She looked at her watch. 'Four o'clock in the afternoon. How do you feel?'

'Well, I've got a headache,' he grimaced. 'And I'm thirsty.'

'A good sign.' The doctor who was in charge of her father's case entered the room, a tall, loose-limbed man of indiscriminate age. His face was young, but his hair was sparse and streaked with grey.

'Good afternoon, Doctor,' Kelly's father greeted

politely. 'Where's that son-on-law of mine?'

'You remember him being here, Daddy?' Kelly said excitedly.

He turned puzzled eyes on her. 'No, I can't say that I do. But it follows that if you're here then so is Jordan. I'm sorry I interrupted your holiday, darling.'

She frowned. 'But, Daddy——'

'Could I examine your father alone, Mrs Lord?' the doctor interrupted. 'You can talk to him in a few minutes. Perhaps you would like to telephone your husband while you're waiting.'

'Oh yes, yes, of course.' She squeezed her father's hand. 'I won't be long, Daddy.'

The telephone at the hotel suite was answered by Janet Amery. 'Mrs Lord?' she acknowledged. 'Yes, Mr Lord is right here,' she said in answer to her query.

'Kelly?' Jordan's sleepy voice came on the other end of the telephone line.

'Resting, Jordan?' Kelly asked bitchily.

'You know damn well I'm not,' he rasped. 'Janet and I have some work to get through.'

I'll bet!' Kelly scorned.

He sighed wearily. 'What do you want, Kelly?'

'Oh, oh yes.' She had momentarily forgotten her reason for calling him on finding him with his beautiful secretary. Janet Amery was quite a nice girl, actually, and yet the intimacy of her relationship with Jordan precluded Kelly becoming friends with her. 'Daddy's awake,' she explained.

'Why the hell didn't you say so in the first place?' he snapped impatiently. 'I'll be there as soon as I can.'

He got there so quickly that he arrived before the doctor had even finished examining her father. 'How is he?' he demanded to know immediately.

'Quite well, actually, although a bit confused.'

'That's only to be expected,' Jordan dismissed, sitting down beside her in the waiting-room.

'I suppose so,' Kelly agreed slowly. 'But he seems to think I've been on holiday.'

'Well, you did just get back from France.'

Kelly didn't ask how he knew that, no doubt he had his sources. 'That wasn't a holiday, Daddy was working the whole of the time we were there.'

Jordan shrugged. 'Confusion, as you said.'

'I'm not so sure——' She broke off to look anxiously at the doctor as he emerged from her father's room.

Jordan stood up. 'Doctor,' he politely shook hands with the other man.

'Mr Lord,' Michael Jones nodded.

Kelly joined then. 'How is he?' she asked eagerly.

'Would you both like to come along to my office?' the doctor invited. 'We can talk more freely there.'

She could barely control her impatience as they all became seated in the ward office. Was there something wrong? Was her father more ill than they had first thought?

The doctor took his time, fiddling idly with the paper-weight on his desk. 'I realise this may seem a strange question,' he said finally. 'But could you tell me how long the two of you have been married?' he spoke to Jordan.

Jordan looked as puzzled at Kelly. 'Five years. Why?'

'Mm, just as I thought,' the doctor nodded, his expression grave.

'What is it?' Kelly's voice was shrill. 'What's wrong?'

'Nothing too serious,' Dr Jones instantly assured her. 'But serious enough. It seems that the bump on your father's head caused slightly more damage than we first suspected.'

'But you said there was no fracture——'

'There isn't, Mrs Lord,' the doctor soothed her. 'You see,' he took a deep breath, 'your father, he—well, he—A few minutes ago he apologised for interrupting your holiday, remember?' he quirked one eyebrow at her.

'Yes,' she nodded frowningly.

He sighed. 'The holiday he referred to was your honeymoon. I'm afraid this bump on his head has caused your father to have a slight lapse of memory.'

'Which means?' Jordan prompted impatiently.

'Which means Mr Darrow has, temporarily we hope, lost five years of his life. As far as he's concerned the two of you have just returned from your honeymoon.'

CHAPTER THREE

KELLY was stunned, speechless. Her father had lost his memory! Well, not all of it, just the relevant part that would tell him she and Jordan were no longer together.

'He has to be told,' she said unthinkingly, looking up at the doctor. 'He'll have to be told that Jordan and I——'

'I doubt it's wise to tell him anything?' Jordan interrupted coldly. 'Am I right, Dr Jones?'

'Quite right, Mr Lord,' the other man nodded gravely. 'At the moment he simply couldn't cope with the knowledge that five years of his life are total blackness to him. His heart condition——'

'Heart condition?' Kelly repeated dazedly. 'I don't know of any——'

'I know,' Jordan acknowledged. 'David told me about it years ago.'

'How many years ago?' she demanded to know.

'About four.' he replied calmly.

Dr Jones nodded. 'That would be about the time he first found out about it.'

'But I wasn't told,' Kelly said dully. 'My father said nothing to me.'

'He probably didn't want to worry you,' the doctor excused. 'After all, he's still a young man, he wouldn't see any necessity for telling you of something that may never happen, to worry you unnecessarily.'

'Now that he's lost his memory he probably doesn't even know about it himself,' she pointed out bitterly.

'I would say it's a certainty that he doesn't, which is all the more reason why he must receive no undue shocks. Normally he knows to avoid any unnecessary stress or strain, without the knowledge of his condition he won't take the necessary precautions, so we must try to protect him all we can.'

'But how long will he be like that?' Kelly sat forward in her seat. 'How long before he remembers?'

The doctor shrugged. 'It could be hours, days, even weeks. I have no way of telling.'

'Weeks?' she echoed. 'But he—In the meantime what do we do?'

'The safest thing is to act as if it really were five years ago. His memory will come back of its own accord, if we try to force the issue it would in all probability make things worse.'

'But we can't—Jordan and I—we don't——'

'What my wife is trying to say,' Jordan cut in dryly, 'is that she and I are separated.'

A ruddy hue coloured the other man's cheeks. 'I see,' he said slowly. 'That makes things a little difficult.'

'In what way?' Jordan's eyes were narrowed.

'Mr Darrow has no other injuries other than the cut on the head. Medically he'll be able to leave hospital in a few days' time. Normally he would go home to you, I wouldn't recommend that he be alone at the moment. But if you're divorced——'

'We aren't divorced,' Jordan put in smoothly. 'Just separated, as I said.'

'I see. Then perhaps it would be possible after all.' He stood up in preparation of ending the meeting. 'I strongly recommend that you seriously consider a temporary reconciliation for Mr Darrow's benefit. Obviously I can only advise you . . .'

'Obviously,' Jordan accepted dryly. 'We'll discuss the problem and let you know what we decide.'

'I'm not going back to living with you,' Kelly told him as soon as they were alone.

'I knew you'd say that,' Jordan said disgustedly, standing up to pace the room. 'As usual you're only thinking of yourself.'

'I'm——'

'You're a selfish little bitch!' he dismissed. 'You always were. You aren't thinking of your father at all, are you? Think what will happen if he suddenly finds out that far from being an ecstatic couple just back from our honeymoon we've in fact lived apart for the past five years.'

An angry flush coloured her cheeks when he called her a selfish bitch, but the rest of what he said basically made sense. '*We* can't turn the clock back,' she said desperately, knowing that she couldn't live with him, especially after responding to that kiss yesterday. She would be leaving herself open to further attacks of that sort.

Jordan's expression was cold and removed. 'I'm not proposing we turn the clock back, I wouldn't want that either. Marrying you at all was sheer madness, I should have had more sense. No, we won't be returning to that, Kelly, but I'm willing to make a show of things for the sake of my friendship with your father. Of course, the ultimate decision lies with you.'

'I—I can't think! I don't want to be with you any more than I have to, and yet—There's my father! I don't want him harmed.'

Jordan's expression was remote. 'You don't have to decide now, I doubt if he'll be discharged for a while.'

'Couldn't you—well, couldn't you go away on business or something?' she looked hopeful.

'That wouldn't be the natural move of a man just back from his honeymoon,' he derided.

'No,' Kelly agreed reluctantly.

Jordan sighed his impatience with her. 'Let's go in and see him now. You can think about this other business later.'

Think about it! She wouldn't be able to do anything else. The last two days of knowing Jordan was here had been bad enough, if she had to actually put on a show of living with him, of loving him, she didn't think she would be able to cope with it. The whole idea of it was ridiculous!

And yet what other solution could there be? At least Jordan was willing to be co-operative, which he didn't have to be. After all, it couldn't be all that convenient for him to suddenly, to all intents and purposes, become a husband again. Janet Amery was just one of the women he would have to explain this strange occurrence to; there could be numerous others. Knowing Jordan there would be.

'Don't think about it now,' he ordered tersely as he looked down at her and saw her pensive expression. 'Try and look the ecstatic bride,' he added derisively.

Her eyes flashed violet. 'I'm trying to remember what it was like to be naïve about you!' she snapped insultingly. 'And I can't think how I could have been taken in by you.'

'I can tell you that in one word, Kelly—sex,' he scorned.

She gasped. 'That's a lie!'

'You enjoyed being made love to,' his gaze ran slowly over her body, his mouth quirked in a humourless smile. 'And I enjoyed making love to you.'

Her eyes sparkled, her mouth set in an angry line. 'For a time,' she nodded. ' Until I bored you. I can't think why you married me.'

'Can't you?' he drawled, casually flicking her dark hair back from her cheek.

'No!' she snapped, flinching away from his long sensitive fingers.

'For a very good reason, Kelly.' He strode out of the office.

She hurriedly followed him, her short legs having trouble keeping pace with his much longer ones. She looked up at him questioningly. 'What was the reason?'

Jordan suddenly stopped dead, causing several other people in the corridor to give them curious looks. 'Now listen, Kelly,' his voice was harsh. 'The time to ask for these explanations was before you walked out on me and our marriage. I certainly don't intend having a post-mortem on it now.'

'Why have you never divorced me, Jordan?'

'Why?' he laughed softly, unpleasantly. 'Quite simply you've proved a valuable deterrent.'

'Deterrent . . .?'

'To any other woman who thought she might like to be my wife,' he explained tauntingly. 'Now smile, my love,' he drawled mockingly. 'We're going in to see your father.'

'But——'

'Smile, Kelly!'

She did so with extreme difficulty, resenting the way he deliberately laced his fingers through hers, the smile of intimacy he gave her as they went into the hospital room.

Her father was very pale, although he brightened somewhat as they came in. 'Did you enjoy Barbados?' his eyes twinkled merrily.

Kelly's blush was perfectly genuine. 'It was very nice,'

she told him in a stilted voice.

Jordan's fingers tightened painfully on hers before he released her hand, putting his arm about her shoulders and pulling her against his side. 'Kelly's shy,' he told her father. 'In actual fact we hardly left our villa,' he smiled down at her, a warning in his eyes.

Her blush deepened. It was true, they hadn't. And she had come back love-drugged, satiated with the possession of Jordan's warm, vibrant body. She had been glowing with love for him—nothing like the wariness with which she now viewed him.

'I think you both forgot to eat,' her father smiled teasingly.

'We had better things to do with our time,' Jordan returned that smile.

Kelly looked at him beneath lowered lashes. He was leaner, quite gaunt in the face, although it in no way detracted from his looks, he would still have those in old age.

'I'm sure you did,' her father chuckled. 'Kelly!' he held out his hands to her.

'Oh, Daddy!' She went down beside him, burying her face in his chest. 'I've been so worried about you,' she sobbed.

He smoothed her hair. 'It's all right, darling, *I'm* all right. And you've had Jordan to lean on.'

Yes, she had. She hadn't felt as lost and alone since Jordan had arrived, although not for one minute would she ever admit that to him. He was an adulterer and she hated him!

'Hey,' her father finally chided, 'you're making my pyjamas all wet!'

'Sorry,' she moved back with a tearful smile.

'I think we should leave your father now, Kelly.' Jordan pulled her up beside him. Let him get some rest.'

'Haven't I been sleeping for five days?' her father grinned.

'Not a restful sleep.' Sister Fellows appeared in the doorway. 'You're still very weak, Mr Darrow, I think it would be as well if your daughter and her husband came back tomorrow.'

'If you say so, Sister.' He turned to wink at Jordan. 'At least I have a beautiful nurse.'

Jordan watched the young woman as she swayed gracefully across the room to begin straightening the bedclothes. 'You do indeed,' he agreed admiringly.

'Come along, darling,' Kelly said with exaggerated sweetness. 'I'm sure we can leave Daddy in Sister Fellows' capable hands.'

Her father hooted with laughter, wincing as it hurt his head. 'You should have been born with green eyes,' he grinned.

Jordan held her firmly against his side, bending his head to kiss her lightly on the lips, his grip tightening as she struggled. 'Kelly knows she has no need to worry about me straying, I'm the typical faithful husband,' he assured her father.

'I should damn well think so,' the other man growled. 'You've only been married a few weeks.'

'Lie still, Mr Darrow,' Sister Fellows told him firmly. 'Or you'll give yourself a colossal headache.'

He grimaced. 'I think I already have.'

Kelly bent to kiss him on the cheek. 'We'll see you in the morning, Daddy.'

'Not too early,' his blue eyes twinkled teasingly. 'I understand from Dr Jones that you've been taking it in turns to sit with me. Spend some time together tomorrow.'

'This is terrible,' Kelly groaned once they were outside in the car. 'I'm not sure if I can keep this up.'

'You're doing fine.' Most of Jordan's attention was on his driving. 'That little show of jealousy convinced him more than anything else. A brilliant piece of acting.'

Except that she hadn't been acting! It was starting all over again, all the bitterness and anger, the burning jealousy that seemed to eat her up. So where did that leave her feelings concerning Jordan? She preferred not to think about it.

'I thought so,' she agreed lightly. 'Although you didn't do too badly yourself.'

'Thanks,' he drawled mockingly. 'I'm a little out of practice, but no doubt I'll soon pick up the habit of the doting husband again.'

'Doting!' Kelly scorned. 'You treated me like an expensive toy.'

'I told you I don't want to discuss the past.' His eyes were a light, icy grey, his jaw rigid. 'From here on in we think of it as the future. As far as your father is concerned that's exactly what it is.'

Her expression became uncertain, her bottom lip trembling slightly. 'You do think he'll get better, don't you?'

'You heard the doctor, the amnesia is only temporary.'

'And when he gets his memory back, how do we explain our living together?'

'We don't,' Jordan said arrogantly. 'I have no need to explain living with my wife to anyone.'

'No one?' she asked disbelievingly.

'No one at all,' he said firmly. 'Can the same be said of you?'

'A boy-friend, you mean?' Kelly flushed.

'That's right,' he nodded.

'No,' she told him jerkily, 'I have no boy-friend.'

She had never had one. She had believed it was because

after Jordan she didn't trust men, but now she wasn't so sure. Maybe the real reason was that she couldn't get Jordan completely out of her system, had felt a loyalty to her marriage even if he hadn't.

'I believe you dated Ian a couple of times after you left me,' Jordan surprised her by saying.

'I would hardly call it dating.' Not when she had spent the whole time talking about Jordan! Ian had always been a good listener, and she liked him, had readily agreed to meet him when he called her a few weeks after she had parted from Jordan. 'I suppose Ian told you we'd met?'

'Yes,' he didn't elaborate.

Kelly licked her lips nervously, shooting him a searching glance, although his bland expression revealed nothing of his inner thoughts. 'What did he say?' she asked with feigned casualness.

Jordan shrugged. 'Just that you had met.'

'Nothing else?'

'No,' came his abrupt reply.

Thank God for that! She had talked to Ian quite openly, although not even to him could she reveal the full extent of Jordan's betrayal. Ian had perhaps known of it anyway—after all, he worked with both Jordan and Angela, might have realised what was going on between his boss and his secretary.

Janet Amery was in their suite when they got back to the hotel. There were papers strewn all over the desk in the lounge, and Janet seemed to be working very hard as she typed out a report, but Kelly still couldn't help wondering if this show wasn't being put on for her benefit.

'Did the call from Burrows come in yet?' Jordan demanded imperiously, striding over to the desk.

'No, Jordan.' Janet looked up from her typing, her eyes a deep clear blue, her complexion perfect, her smart silky suit the perfect outfit for the perfect secretary.

'Damn him,' Jordan muttered. 'Doesn't he realise I need those figures before I go ahead with this deal?'

'I'm sure he does,' Janet soothed.

'Get him on the phone again,' he ordered tersely. 'Hell, Jimmy is only keeping my option open until ten tonight.'

'Excuse me,' Kelly said softly, knowing of old that air of excitement about Jordan. He thrived on work, continued with his wheeling and dealing even though he had enough money to last him ten lifetimes. 'I'm going to my room.'

Jordan turned to look at her, as if for a few minutes he had forgotten her very existence. 'You'll join me for dinner?'

'I don't think so,' she shook her head. 'You appear to be rather busy.'

'I still have to eat,' he dismissed abruptly.

'I wouldn't want to intrude,' a trace of bitterness entered her voice. 'I'm sure you and Miss Amery don't need me around. I'll eat in my room.'

Jordan strode over to her, grasping her arm and pushing her roughly out into the corridor of their suite. 'You'll damn well eat with me,' his eyes glittered angrily. 'And you can cut the remarks about Janet and myself, I think her fiancé might have something to say about them.'

Kelly's eyes widened. 'She's engaged?'

He nodded, his expression mocking. 'To my personal assistant.'

'Burrows?'

'That right.'

'Then it wasn't very polite of you to talk about him that way to Miss Amery.' A feeling of relief rushed through her, and she made every effort to hide it from Jordan. If he should ever realise that her jealousy over Janet Amery and Sister Fellows was real, very real, she would die of embarrassment.

'I don't approve of those sort of relationships in business,' he said haughtily. 'It isn't conducive to work.'

'And nothing must interfere with your work, must it?' Kelly scorned, her head tilted back. 'I'm surprised you bother any more, after all you're rich enough already.'

'Haven't you heard, it's a good substitute.' His mouth twisted.

She frowned. 'For what?'

'This!' With a groan his mouth claimed hers for the third time in two days, if anything his hunger increased, his open mouth devouring all her resistance.

His hands were firm on her back, although Kelly needed no force to keep her against him, feeling as helpless as metal pulled to a magnet. Her neck was arched, her feet almost off the ground with the force of his embrace.

His lips moved against hers with fierce insistence, demanding that she meet his passion in full, unrelenting as she began to gasp for air. She felt lightheaded, dizzy, and she refused to put this down to anything but her breathlessness, refused to acknowledge the fire in her veins, the fever in her eyes.

'Put me down!' she demanded indignantly, knowing her mouth must be bare of lip-gloss, her hair tumbled about her face.

'Certainly.' He lowered her to the ground, although there was strength enough in him to ignore her command and carry her off to one of the four bedrooms in this suite if he should care to. Kelly told herself she would have fought such a move, but she also knew it was a fight she would have lost.

Anger burnt at his ability to look unmoved by the passion and desire he had just forced from her. 'Don't ever to that again!'

Jordan gave a soft laugh, his expression lazily mocking. 'But I told you, I like kissing you.'

'And I hate it!' She glared at him.

'Liar!' he taunted. 'You love it, you always did.'

'I thought we weren't going to discuss the past,' she said stiffly, her face bright red with shame. Jordan was too experienced not to know she had surrendered to him completely a few minutes ago.

'But, Kelly,' he mocked throatily, 'that wasn't the past.'

'It wasn't the future either,' she snapped.

'It was here and now, and you liked it as much as I did. Besides, we should get in some practice.'

'P-practice . . .?'

'Well, it won't look very good in front of your father if I don't even know how to kiss my wife. You might have learnt to kiss differently since last we met.'

Her eyes flashed with anger. 'And how would I have done—Ooh!' she cried at his smile of satisfaction. 'I've been out with other men,' she told him defiantly.

'But apparently none of them for long enough for them to have kissed you,' he drawled, straightening the cuff of his shirt beneath the navy blue suit he wore.

'I've been kissed!' She almost stamped her foot with rage.

Jordan's rage was even fiercer than hers, deep lines grooved beside his nose and mouth. 'By how many?' he asked tightly.

'A few,' she refused to meet the demand of his gaze. 'Not as many women as you've had, I'm sure.'

His fingers bit into her arms, and Kelly felt sure they would leave bruises. 'We aren't discussing me, Kelly. How many men have there been? Have you slept with any of them?'

She was white with shock, hardly able to stand as he shook her. 'Certainly not! Can you say the same about your women?' she challenged as he at last let her go.

He watched her between narrowed lids, his eyes a metallic grey. 'And if I can?'

Kelly gave a scornful snort. 'After five years?' she

derided, a smile on her lips. 'You couldn't go for five days without a woman, let alone five years!'

'Maybe not,' he shrugged, his anger apparently forgotten.

'If you're looking for a reason to divorce me, Jordan, you won't find one that way.'

'After this amount of time we could claim incompatibility. But I've already told you I don't want a divorce.'

'Of course, a wife in the background suits you.'

'Exactly,' he nodded, completely in control again. 'Do you want a divorce? Is there someone you want to marry?'

She frowned. 'No.'

'And you don't want children, so——'

'Who says I don't?' she cut in sharply.

'You did.' His gaze was tense.

'When——? That was before,' she realised what he meant. 'I was upset at the time, confused. I didn't know what I was saying.'

'You knew you were telling me you hated me,' he recalled bitterly. 'You knew it, and you enjoyed watching me crumple. What do you think it did to me having you say you hated me when we'd just lost our child?'

'*My* child,' she corrected vehemently, remembering all too well the reason she had lost it, remembering him with Angela Divine. 'It was never your child, Jordan. For all the interest you took of it—her,' she amended bitterly, 'she might as well not have existed.'

'You don't understand,' he shook his head wearily. 'You never did.'

'No. It's strange, isn't it?' You see, I always thought a husband was very interested in the existence of his child. I was going to call her Jordana, you know.' Her eyes flashed with dislike. 'Thank God she was never born and named after a bastard like you!'

His hand shot out and hit her hard across one cheek, and her head reeled back from the blow. 'Oh God!' he groaned as she stared at him with tear-filled, accusing eyes. '*God*!' he groaned again, his face buried in his hands. 'Now what have you made me do?' he muttered in an agonised voice. 'Kelly——'

'Don't touch me!' She stepped back as he reached out. 'Don't come near me!'

'Kelly——'

'No!' She turned on her heel and ran into her bedroom, turning the key in the lock before leaning heavily back against the door.

'Kelly!' the muffled sound of his voice came through the door. 'Kelly, I'm sorry. Open the door, darling.'

'No!' she answered in a shaky voice, her cheek stinging.

She heard him sigh. 'I didn't mean to frighten you. For God's sake let me in so I can explain.' He rattled the door-handle. 'Let me in, Kelly.'

'I said no and I meant no!' she told him vehemently.

'Okay!' he snapped, his patience having run out. 'If that's the way you want it. I'll order dinner for eight-thirty, make sure you aren't late.'

'I'm not dining with you,' she gasped.

'Try not being there and see what happens,' he said threateningly, his firm tread moving away.

Kelly moved over to the bed, her legs feeling shaky as she slowly sank down on to the mattress. Jordan had hit her! No one had ever hit her before, not her father, no one, and to say she had been shocked by the action was an understatement.

But she had deserved it! She had deserved much more than that. How could she have said such a cruel thing to him? Only with Jordan had she ever lost her temper so completely, her emotions were always in the extreme where he was concerned. She had put him up on a pedestal, and because he wasn't able to share her enthusiasm for the baby the foundations to that pedestal had started to rock. She hadn't allowed for the fact that not all men want children, that some even disliked them. She could have sworn Jordan wasn't one of those men, but his instant aversion to touching her and his turning to another woman had more than proved that he was.

Now how could she prepare to have dinner with him this evening as if that slap had never happened? Things had been strained before, but surely they were impossible now.

After soaking in the bath for an hour she took a look at her face. There was a slight discolouration and swelling to her bottom lip, the marks of Jordan's fingers starting to fade now. She had been aghast when she had first looked at it, shocked at the livid marks on her face. Skilful make-up covered the last of these marks, although there was nothing she could do about her bruised and swollen lip, her lip-gloss just seemed to emphasise it.

Her gown was pastel green, very figure-hugging, cling-ing to her narrow waist. It gave her a look of coolness, of sophistication, and made her eyes deeply violet, her hair even blacker, and gave her skin a wonderful honey tone.

Dinner would be served at eight-thirty, Jordan had said, so she made her entrance at exactly eight twenty-five, sure that Jordan would be no more eager than she was to indulge in light conversation.

He was already in the lounge when she came in, sitting in one of the armchairs, his expression morose as he swirled some whisky around in his glass. Kelly knew it was whisky, Jordan never drank anything else. The room was also filled with the aroma of his cheroots.

He stood up as soon as he saw her, his suit cream, the collar of the black shirt he wore beneath it turned back over his jacket. His hair was newly washed, very dark and springy, and as he moved forward Kelly could smell his tangy aftershave.

Jordan's dark gaze searched her pale features. 'I've

telephoned the hospital,' he told her huskily. 'You father is sleeping comfortably.'

'Thank you,' she accepted coolly.

'Kelly . . .' he groaned, grasping her hands in his. 'Can you ever forgive me?'

'There's nothing to forgive,' she extricated her hands moving away from him. 'If I ever say anything like that to you again I hope you'll deal with me in the same way. Could I have a sherry, please?' she changed the subject.

'We can't just dismiss it like that,' he poured her sherry for her. 'You mouth, your beautiful mouth!' He shut his eyes as if wishing he could shut out the memory of that painful scene. 'It must hurt like hell.'

Kelly flinched as he would have touched her, rescuing her sherry from his shaking fingers. 'It will remind me in future to keep it shut,' she said lightly. She smiled as a knock sounded on the main door, wishing an end to this conversation. 'That will be our dinner—I hope. I'm very hungry. What did you order for me?'

'Duck.'

Her eyes glowed. 'My favourite.'

'Still?' he quirked his eyebrows.

'Yes.'

'It's nice to know some of your tastes haven't changed.' He moved to answer the door.

The waiter stayed to serve them their food and wine, making anything but general conversation impossible, so at least Kelly was able to eat her meal in peace.

She poured their coffee in the lounge, the waiter having wheeled away the service trolley. 'I've been thinking, Jordan,' she sipped her coffee.

'Mm?' He was relaxing in the chair opposite her, his long legs stretched out in front of him.

Kelly nodded, trying not to notice how attractive he looked, that wary look having left his face now. She could almost believe they were the happily married couple they were trying to appear—and that wouldn't do at all. She must keep up her guard against Jordan, he had already shown he wasn't averse to kissing her when the mood took him. 'It's about the house,' she hastily explained.

Jordan frowned his puzzlement. 'Your father has a housekeeper, doesn't he?'

'Oh yes,' she dismissed, automatically passing him the sugar. Sugar and cakes were Jordan's weakness, and yet he didn't put on an ounce of weight. 'I didn't mean Daddy's house, I meant ours.'

'What about it?'

'We don't have one. And Daddy's sure to remember the house, we spent months decorating it before I moved in. He's going to think it strange if we bring him back here. I suppose we could always rent an apartment, but——'

'Not necessary,' Jordan cut in lazily.

'But we can't go back to his house either, he didn't have it then. Don't you remember——'

'I still have the house, Kelly.'

Her eyes widened. '*Our* house?'

'That's right,' he nodded.

'And Mrs McLeod? Do you still have her too?' Kelly asked dazedly.

'Yes.'

'But why?' She shook her head. 'What I mean is, why stay here when our house isn't far away?'

'You want the truth?'

'Of course,' she said indignantly.

'Memories,' came Jordan's single-worded reply.

'Memories . . .? Good or bad?' she asked sharply.

'Oh, definitely——' he broke off as someone knocked on the door. 'Excuse me.' He stood up to answer it.

Kelly could have cried with frustration. She had wanted to know the answer to that question, so when she saw it was Janet Amery at the door she glared at her angrily.

The poor girl couldn't have missed that show of resentment, and she moved uncomfortably. 'I'm sorry to trouble you, Jordan, Mrs Lord,' she said nervously. 'But Richard just called.'

'And?' Jordan was charged with a sudden excitement.

Janet held out a sheet of paper to him. 'I have the figures here.'

He took the sheet from her, skimming over it. There was a look of triumph in his eyes when he at last looked up. 'Get Jimmy on the phone,' he instructed. 'And when you've done that have Richard stand by. I'll have some last-minute instructions for him.'

'Yes, Jordan.' She was already moving to the phone.

'On second thoughts don't have Richard stand by, get him over here,' Jordan said thoughtfully. 'We can discuss the finer points of the contract once I've spoken to Jimmy.'

'Yes, Jordan.' His secretary began to dial, giving a look of apology in Kelly's direction. 'I'm sorry I've spoilt your evening,' she said shyly.

'You haven't.' Kelly stood up resignedly, turning to Jordan. 'I think I'll say goodnight.'

'Goodnight?' He looked up from the figures he was working on. 'Oh—oh yes, Goodnight, Kelly.'

She didn't think he even noticed her going. It was just like old times, nothing had changed. Except her. She had changed. Once upon a time she would have made a scene about his preoccupation with work. But then she had been his wife, now she was just playing a role, and the sooner she remembered that the better.

How long would it last? How long would they have to continue this charade? It was becoming more difficult by the minute, Kelly having extreme difficulty remembering she was only playing a part, that in the end she and Jordan would once again be apart.

CHAPTER FOUR

THEY visited her father daily, either together or individually, but he didn't seem to have remembered any more, treating Kelly and Jordan to a lot of teasing about their newly married state. Kelly preferred it when she saw her father alone, finding it a strain to behave like a blushing bride when in the company of Jordan. Alone she could recall how happy she had really been, and her father seemed convinced.

She went to the house the day before her father's discharge, just to make sure everything was ready for when they arrived. Besides, she had to reintroduce herself to Mrs McLeod; the poor woman must be in a complete daze about this strange turn of events.

Nothing had changed, none of the decor, nor Mrs McLeod's plump, bustling figure, nothing. Kelly could almost believe herself that the last five years away from Jordan hadn't happened. She was falling more and more into this trap even at the hotel, was accepting Jordan's easy companionship, was even coming to rely on it.

'Here we are, then,' Mrs McLeod brought Kelly in a tray of tea. 'It's just like old times,' she beamed.

'Not quite,' Kelly smiled. 'I actually came just to make sure Jordan had explained the situation to you.'

'Oh, Mr Lord has told me all about your father. Terrible business, terrible.' She shook her head.

'Yes,' Kelly agreed. 'Won't you join me in some tea?' she invited.

The elderly lady flushed her pleasure. 'Oh, I couldn't!'

'Sure?' Kelly poured herself a cup.

'Yes—thank you. I've put your father in the room he always used, I thought that best.'

'Yes,' Kelly frowned. 'It's all going to be very awkward, like walking on broken glass.'

'He doesn't remember a thing?'

'Not after Mr Lord and I were married, no. That's the reason it's all going to be awkward.'

Just how awkward she didn't realise until she and Jordan brought her father home the next day. Now they would be continually under her father's watchful gaze, wouldn't be able to drop their pose for a minute. Dr Jones had underlined the fact that her father must receive no shocks, had direly warned of the possible consequences if he realised the truth, desecrated the black void in his memory.

Her father looked around him admiringly as he seated himself in the lounge, the small plaster on his brow the only evidence of his recent accident. 'I always liked this house,' he spoke to Jordan. 'But you have to admit that Kelly's made it into a home.'

'She certainly has,' Jordan nodded agreement, watching Kelly as she sat pleating her skirt. 'I wouldn't know what to do without her now.'

'I should hope not,' the other man laughed. 'Not for a while anyway. How are you, Kelly? You're looking a little pale.'

'Darling?' Jordan prompted as she continued the nervous movements on her skirt.

She looked startled, colour flooding her cheeks at how easy he found it to use that endearment. 'Sorry?' she blinked her puzzlement.

His mouth twisted wryly. 'Your father was expressing concern about your paleness.'

She bit her lip. 'Excitement,' she excused jerkily. 'It's so nice to have you home, Daddy.'

'It's nice to be here. I was just wondering if your paleness could be due to——anything?' He quirked an eyebrow questioningly.

'Due to any——? No!' Kelly went white. 'No . . .' she repeated faintly.

'Give us a chance, David,' Jordan took over. 'We've only been married a few weeks.'

'It was just an idea——'

'Excuse me.' Kelly jumped to her feet. 'I—I feel ill!' She ran from the room.

Her father had unwittingly touched on the one subject she couldn't act over. She was shaking by the time she reached the bedroom she had once shared with Jordan, sinking down on to the bed before her legs gave out on her. A baby was the one thing she couldn't pretend about.

The bedroom door opened and Jordan came into the room. 'That wasn't very wise.'

'Wise!' she repeated shrilly. 'I know it wasn't,' the fight went out of her. 'But I couldn't—I couldn't take that, Jordan. Not about the baby. Try to understand, Jordan——'

'I do understand,' he cut in gently, coming over to sit beside her on the double bed. 'I do understand, Kelly,' he took her hand into his.

Her breath caught in her throat. So far she had avoided letting him touch her as much as possible. Here in this bedroom, where so many intimacies had taken place between them, it was all the more dangerous.

'You've never understood, Jordan,' she dismissed scathingly, snatching her hand away. 'Now isn't the time to start trying.'

'I'm not going to argue with you.' He stood up to pace the room. 'Not with your father waiting for us downstairs.'

'No,' she accepted quietly. 'I'm sorry.'

His eyes widened fractionally. 'Come down and talk to your father. He's going to have a rest after lunch, so you can relax for a while. I never realised you found it such a strain being in love with me.'

'*Pretending* to be in love with you. There's a subtle difference.'

'It isn't subtle, Kelly,' his mouth twisted. 'It's like a blow on the head.'

'Maybe.'

Anger blazed in his steely grey eyes at her indifference. 'I shall be working this afternoon while your father is sleeping. What will you be doing?'

Kelly shrugged uninterestedly. 'I'll stay here, I suppose. One of us should be here, don't you think?' Her voice was sugary sweet in her sarcasm.

'Are you spoiling for that argument after all, Kelly?' Jordan's voice was soft, threateningly so.

'I was just pointing out——'

'I shall be here all afternoon,' he interrupted icily. 'Janet and I will be working in my study.'

Jealousy flared and was quickly dampened down. 'In that case I'll go out.' She had watched Jordan with his secretary these last few days, had watched the lazy way he flirted with her, had seen the way the other girl blushed at his light bantering. It wasn't the reaction of a girl who was completely uninterested in him, although she and Richard Burrows seemed happy enough.

Kelly had met Richard Burrows several times at the hotel, had found him pleasant enough, although he didn't have Ian Smythe's ability to make decisions for himself. Jordan was still very much in charge of his business empire, Richard more in the nature of another secretary rather than the assistant he was supposed to be. Ian had always taken on more responsibility, in fact during the first months of their marriage Jordan had left a lot of work to the other man, spending most of his time with Kelly—until she had told him about the baby. Then he had gone back to the office, had taken to working long into the evening too, had often not even arrived home before Kelly had gone to bed.

'Kelly,' Jordan stopped her as she moved to the door. 'Kelly, as far as your father is concerned our marriage is just starting, couldn't we do the same?'

Her violet eyes searched his face in questioning disbelief. 'Are you suggesting we start again?' she asked stiffly.

'Yes,' he confirmed huskily.

She flinched away from him, glaring her dislike. 'You don't need a wife, Jordan, you never did.'

There was a white ring of tension about his mouth. 'I need you, Kelly,' his voice was husky. 'Only you.'

'It's a little late in the day to discover that,' she told him coldly. 'Now if you don't mind I think I'll go down and talk to my father. We aren't being very good hosts. Are you coming down?'

'In a minute.' He didn't look at her, his hands clenched into fists at his sides. 'I'll be down in a minute,' he repeated jerkily.

'Very well,' Kelly left him.

If she had been weaker, if she didn't have that conversation between Jordan and Angela Divine to remind her of his duplicity she might, almost, have been persuaded by his plea for a second chance. But if he could betray her once then he could do it again, and she wasn't strong enough to leave him a second time.

Her father was drinking coffee when she entered the lounge, a weariness to him in repose that he made every effort to hide when with Jordan and herself. He looked older, with deep lines beside his nose and mouth; he had lost weight too, and Kelly's heart went out to him.

ever coming to an exchange of abuse.'

'That's because you weren't here. It was after you did your disappearing act. She didn't realise you'd left me.'

'I see. And she called you—that?'

'Yes,' Jordan confirmed. 'So you should have an enjoyable afternoon.'

She smiled. 'It would appear so. I'll be back in time for dinner.' She looked pointedly at his hand resting on the open door. 'Would you mind?'

'Certainly,' and he stepped back.

Kelly's mouth tightened as the familiar red Mini came down the driveway. 'Your—secretary has arrived,' she told Jordan tightly.

He smiled. 'So she has.'

'I'm so glad you won't be lonely.' Kelly's sarcasm was unmistakable.

'I'm never that, not unless I choose to be.'

'I can believe that,' she snapped, slamming the car door and accelerating swiftly out of the driveway, nodding cool acknowledgement of Janet Amery's friendly wave. No doubt the other woman would enjoy her afternoon alone with Jordan.

Kelly's foot went down harder on the accelerator. So Maggie had seen Jordan after she had left him? Strange that she had never mentioned the meeting. Maybe she just hadn't wanted to upset her.

Maggie had been her friend since schooldays, the daughter of a rich American cattle baron and his English wife, and she had been sent to England for her education. Maggie had found England more to her liking, hating her father's ranch and all the hard work that went with it. Apparently her father had been hoping for a boy, and when it was found his wife could have no more children he had brought Maggie up to follow in his footsteps, insisting she learn the workings of the ranch from the bottom

He turned and saw her, and the ill look instantly disappeared. 'I'm sorry, darling,' he stood up to come over and put his arm about her shoulders. 'Jordan explained to me that a baby is a sensitive subject to you right now, that he'd already been unreasonable about it by asking you to start a family straight away. I agree with you, darling, eighteen is far too young to be a mother.'

Anger blazed within her at Jordan's excuse for her behaviour to her father. How dared he make it seem that she was the one who objected to having a family when he was the one——! 'Much too young, Daddy,' she agreed tightly.

Over lunch Kelly was brittlely gay, fooling her father, but not fooling Jordan for a moment. She ignored his studied glances, and talked happily to her father, leaving the house as soon as her father had gone to his room to rest.

'Where are you going?' Jordan caught up with her just as she was getting into her car.

'Into town.' She got in behind the wheel, fastening her seat-belt. 'I told you I was going out.'

Jordan still held the car door open. '*Where* are you going? And don't say into town again. I want to know exactly where in London you're going.'

Kelly looked up at him with glittering violet eyes. 'I'm going to see Maggie. I take it you do remember Maggie?'

His mouth twisted. 'Very well.'

Kelly's expression was one of taunting enjoyment. 'I can see that you do.'

'We always disliked each other intensely.'

'Yes,' she agreed with satisfaction.

'I take it that's why you choose to visit her. You can both sit and agree what a selfish bastard I am. I think that was what she called me the last time we met.'

Kelly frowned. 'When was that? I don't remember it

'No,' she accepted quietly. 'I'm sorry.'

His eyes widened fractionally. 'Come down and talk to your father. He's going to have a rest after lunch, so you can relax for a while. I never realised you found it such a strain being in love with me.'

'*Pretending* to be in love with you. There's a subtle difference.'

'It isn't subtle, Kelly,' his mouth twisted. 'It's like a blow on the head.'

'Maybe.'

Anger blazed in his steely grey eyes at her indifference. 'I shall be working this afternoon while your father is sleeping. What will you be doing?'

Kelly shrugged uninterestedly. 'I'll stay here, I suppose. One of us should be here, don't you think?' Her voice was sugary sweet in her sarcasm.

'Are you spoiling for that argument after all, Kelly?' Jordan's voice was soft, threateningly so.

'I was just pointing out——'

'I shall be here all afternoon,' he interrupted icily. 'Janet and I will be working in my study.'

Jealousy flared and was quickly dampened down. 'In that case I'll go out.' She had watched Jordan with his secretary these last few days, had watched the lazy way he flirted with her, had seen the way the other girl blushed at his light bantering. It wasn't the reaction of a girl who was completely uninterested in him, although she and Richard Burrows seemed happy enough.

Kelly had met Richard Burrows several times at the hotel, had found him pleasant enough, although he didn't have Ian Smythe's ability to make decisions for himself. Jordan was still very much in charge of his business empire, Richard more in the nature of another secretary rather than the assistant he was supposed to be. Ian had always taken on more responsibility, in fact during the

first months of their marriage Jordan had left a lot of
work to the other man, spending most of his time with
Kelly—until she had told him about the baby. Then he
had gone back to the office, had taken to working long
into the evening too, had often not even arrived home
before Kelly had gone to bed.

'Kelly,' Jordan stopped her as she moved to the door.
'Kelly, as far as your father is concerned our marriage is
just starting, couldn't we do the same?'

Her violet eyes searched his face in questioning disbelief.
'Are you suggesting we start again?' she asked stiffly.

'Yes,' he confirmed huskily.

She flinched away from him, glaring her dislike. 'You
don't need a wife, Jordan, you never did.'

There was a white ring of tension about his mouth. 'I
need you, Kelly,' his voice was husky. 'Only you.'

'It's a little late in the day to discover that,' she told
him coldly. 'Now if you don't mind I think I'll go down
and talk to my father. We aren't being very good hosts.
Are you coming down?'

'In a minute.' He didn't look at her, his hands clenched
into fists at his sides. 'I'll be down in a minute,' he repeated
jerkily.

'Very well,' Kelly left him.

If she had been weaker, if she didn't have that conversation between Jordan and Angela Divine to remind her
of his duplicity she might, almost, have been persuaded
by his plea for a second chance. But if he could betray her
once then he could do it again, and she wasn't strong
enough to leave him a second time.

Her father was drinking coffee when she entered the
lounge, a weariness to him in repose that he made every
effort to hide when with Jordan and herself. He looked
older, with deep lines beside his nose and mouth; he had
lost weight too, and Kelly's heart went out to him.

up. Maggie had stuck it for a year before coming back to England and staying. Unlike Kelly she had never married, although she never lacked for partners.

Jordan had taken an instant dislike to the other girl, claiming she was far too free and easy with her favours. He refused to meet Maggie socially, and if Kelly had wanted to see her friend she had always had to meet her at a restaurant or at Maggie's flat. That Maggie disliked Jordan too she didn't even try to hide, and Kelly had found their animosity disturbing.

When she called Maggie the other girl was luckily able to take time out from her freelance fashion designing to meet Kelly for afternoon tea. They hadn't seen each other for months, and Kelly's mood lightened as soon as she saw the vivaceous Maggie enter the restaurant. Auburn hair, feathered into curling tendrils down her back, deep brown eyes fringed by dark lashes, a snub nose sprinkled lightly with freckles, her mouth wide and smiling, Maggie was one of the most naturally beautiful women Kelly had ever seen. She wore her self-designed clothes with a grace that drew attention to their flamboyant lines. At the moment she had on a tiered dress in blue and purple, the bodice very tight, but suiting her tiny bust. She had the model's perfect figure, and Kelly had often envied her her tall lissom body and slender curves.

'Kelly!' Maggie launched herself into her arms, finally moving back to hold her at arm's length. 'My, you're looking well!'

Kelly smiled back at her. 'So are you.'

'I heard about your father,' Maggie sobered. 'But I only got back from the States yesterday, and when I called the house they refused to tell me where you were. I'm so glad you called this afternoon or I might have had to go to the police.'

Kelly bit her lip. 'There's a reason for the secrecy.'

Maggie's brown gaze sharpened. 'Do tell! It sounds as if it might be interesting.'

The whole story came out, haltingly at first, and then in a rush. 'So now we just have to wait,' she finished with a sigh.

'And in the meantime you're having to live with Jordan?' Maggie sounded scandalised.

Kelly laughed at her expression. 'He is still my husband, Maggie,' she smiled.

'You mean you and he—that you—you're back, *together*?' Maggie wrinkled her nose in disgust.

'No!' Kelly's voice was sharp. 'No, I don't mean that. I was just pointing out that there's no legal reason why we shouldn't be living together.'

'I don't suppose the legalities of it would have bothered Jordan, anyway.'

'I don't suppose they would.' Jordan had always been a law unto himself.

'He probably wouldn't even have got married if he could have got you any other way.'

'Maggie!' Kelly gasped.

'Well, would he?'

'I don't know, maybe not,' she accepted dully.

'You always were naïve, Kelly.' Maggie helped herself to one of the delicately cut sandwiches they had ordered with their tea, biting into it hungrily. Maggie was always hungry, was one of those people who could eat and eat and not put on a pound. 'Now, me, I would have just slept with him and saved myself all that heartache.'

'At the time I didn't realise there would be all that heartache.' Kelly ignored the sandwiches and cakes, just sipping her tea.

'Jordan isn't the sort of man for the "happy ever after" scene,' Maggie scorned. 'He likes a brief affair, and then it's over.'

Kelly bristled with indignation, for once Maggie's condemnation of Jordan irritating her. 'Considering you don't even like my husband you profess to know a lot about him,' she snapped.

'Oh dear,' Maggie drawled, sounding very American in that moment. 'Have I roused the slumbering tiger?'

'What do you mean?' Kelly asked curtly.

'I always remember at school,' Maggie helped herself to another sandwich, 'it took a lot to make you angry, you were always such a quiet little thing, and yet when your temper did go you usually roared, as you're doing now.'

Kelly looked shamefaced. She had always received nothing but kindness from Maggie. Okay, so she made her dislike of Jordan known, but he was no less insulting about her. 'I'm sorry, Maggie,' she said ruefully. 'As you can imagine, it's all a bit tense at home at the moment.'

'I can imagine,' Maggie instantly agreed. 'And Jordan's perfectly happy to live in such—sterility?'

Kelly blushed at Maggie's plain speaking. 'I would doubt he's doing that.'

'When did he ever?' her friend nodded. 'But he doesn't mind this arrangement?'

'He was the one who insisted on it.'

'Oh dear!'

Kelly's look was sharp. 'Why did you say "oh dear" like that? We didn't really have any choice.'

'Jordan is never pushed into doing anything he doesn't want to. Has he tried to get you into bed with him yet?'

'Maggie! Isn't that a little too personal?' Her face was fiery red.

'Maybe. But has he?'

'No,' Kelly snapped.

Maggie raised one finely plucked eyebrow. 'You sound a bit peeved.'

'Don't be silly,' Kelly said sharply. 'I just don't like your line of questioning.'

Her friend shrugged goodnaturedly. 'I only asked because I remember you hardly ever used to be out of bed.'

Maggie was a dear, and Kelly loved her very much, but she didn't care for this conversation at all.

'Maggie——'

'Okay, okay,' Maggie helped herself to a cream cake now. 'I do love this English habit of afternoon tea.' She grinned. 'It gives me an excuse to make a pig of myself in between meals too. I like elevenses as well.'

'You'll get fat!'

'Not me,' Maggie laughed. 'At school they used to call me Olive Oyl, remember, but I'm glad now that I'm so skinny. Every woman who sees me in one of my own creations thinks that she's going to look the same, even if she's the size of an elephant. No, really, Kelly,' she insisted as Kelly began to laugh. 'Now I'm not boasting, but I look marvellous in my own clothes, and—Stop it, Kelly! Now stop laughing,' she chided reproachfully. 'I'm being serious.'

'I know,' Kelly chuckled. 'Without boasting,' she teased.

'Well . . .' Maggie grinned back at her. 'Maybe I was a bit.'

'You were,' Kelly nodded, her eyes twinkling merrily.

'And so I ought. You never get anywhere in this world without grabbing what you want. I had to learn that the hard way. When I came back to England and Dad cut off my allowance I decided I was going to survive without his help. It hasn't always been easy, but at least now I'm keeping my head above water. Dad even started to mellow some while I was home this time. He was talking of opening a boutique for me.'

'Oh, I am glad!' Kelly knew how Maggie's father's

attitude had hurt her over the years.

'In the States,' she added with a grimace.

'Oh. Don't you want that?'

'I like England, especially at the moment. I have a lovely new guy.' She shrugged. 'Right now I don't want to leave him. In a couple of months I could feel differently, but right now, no. And speaking of him,' she gave a hurried look at her wrist-watch, 'I have to go now, I'm cooking him dinner.'

'*You* are?' Kelly had never known Maggie boil a kettle unless she really had to.

'Crazy, isn't it?' Maggie pulled a face. 'He's the first guy I ever did that for.'

'Must be serious,' Kelly smiled.

'Maybe.' Maggie stood up. 'I'll have to love you and leave you, Kelly. I'll give you a call, hmm?'

'You do that. I want to hear more about this superman who has you tied to the cooker.'

'It hasn't gone that far yet. Besides, he was ill for a week last time I cooked for him.'

'Then I'm surprised he trusts you again.'

'So am I.' Maggie blew Kelly a kiss. 'Be good,' came her parting shot.

Kelly always felt the same after being with Maggie—as if she had just passed through a whirlpool! Her friend had boundless energy for everything, and never entered into anything half-heartedly.

She drank her own tea at a leisurely pace, in no hurry to get back to the house. Her father would be resting until dinner time, and she had no wish to be alone with Jordan any longer than she needed to.

When a woman walking past her table tripped and almost fell Kelly was the first to her feet to steady her. That the woman was beautiful was indisputable, that she was also very pregnant was also indisputable.

'Are you all right?' Kelly asked concernedly.

'I'm fine, thank you,' the voice was cool and very refined. 'Just a little dizzy, that's all.'

'Here, sit down.' Kelly pulled out a chair for her. 'Shall I pour you a cup of tea? It would take away the dizziness,' she encouraged as the other girl seemed about to refuse.

'Very well—thank you.' The girl was very white. 'I was waiting for my husband, but he seems to have been delayed.'

'Never mind,' Kelly poured out the tea. 'Sugar?'

'No, thanks. This is very kind of you,' the girl smiled shyly.

She had short blonde curls and laughing blue eyes. Kelly liked her immediately. 'Not kind at all. I can imagine how you must be feeling.'

The girl blushed prettily, and looked at the wedding ring on Kelly's finger. 'Do you have children of your own?'

'No.' Kelly paled. 'Almost. But it didn't work out.'

'Oh, I am sorry,' the blue eyes were warm with compassion. 'They've made such advances in this field, and yet I almost lost this baby in the beginning too. My name is Laura, by the way.'

'Kelly,' she supplied.

'I'm pleased to meet you, Kelly. I was feeling lonely, so I appreciate your talking to me. My husband is often busy, I suppose that's why he's been delayed today.'

'I know the feeling,' Kelly grimaced.

'Is your husband the same?'

'He never stops.' She felt she could be forgiven calling Jordan her husband, technically he was still that. 'When is the baby due?' She knew it couldn't be long.

'Another five weeks,' Laura smiled coyly. 'I feel like a pumpkin at the moment!'

'It will soon be over.'

'And then I'll have the dirty nappies and the crying to cope with. I didn't mean it,' Laura laughed. 'I'm very excited really. And my husband . . .! You would think no one else ever had a baby.'

'That's nice.' There was an emotional catch in Kelly's voice. If only Jordan had reacted like that, instead of turning away from her.

'Yes.' Laura's face lit up. 'Here he comes now.' She stood up, her eyes glowing. 'Darling!' She launched herself into the arms of her husband.

'Sorry I'm late, darling.' He held her at arm's length, smiling proudly down at her.

'Business?' she chided teasingly.

'How did you guess!'

Kelly recognised that voice, knew the man who was Laura's husband. 'Ian!' she cried her pleasure, standing up too. 'Ian Smythe!'

He turned puzzled blue eyes on her for several seconds. 'Kelly?' he said uncertainly. 'Kelly, is that you?'

'None other,' she beamed at him.

'My God—Kelly!' He hugged her to him, looking just as she remembered him, dark blond hair, laughing blue eyes, lean and muscular. 'It's good to see you again,' he grinned.

'And you.'

'I take it you two have met before,' Laura interrupted them coolly, eyeing them suspiciously.

Ian's arm went about his wife's shoulders. 'Let's go through to the lounge, we seem to be attracting rather a lot of attention standing here. I just can't believe it's you, Kelly. After all this time.'

'Perhaps you would care to introduce me, Ian,' his wife said icily as they seated themselves in the lounge.

'I'm sorry,' he looked startled. 'I thought you must know each other.'

His wife explained how she and Kelly had come to be

sitting together, Ian expressing his concern. 'Don't fuss,' Laura told him. 'I'm perfectly all right.'

'Yes, but——'

'She really is okay, Ian,' Kelly soothed, noticing that Laura was becoming agitated, and in her condition that could only do harm.

'Well . . . if you say so,' he accepted grudgingly.

'The introduction, Ian,' his wife reminded him.

'Oh yes, yes, of course. Laura, this is Kelly Lord. Kelly, my wife Laura.'

Laura smiled tightly. 'That wasn't much of an introduction, darling. How do you know Mrs Lord—Lord?' she repeated slowly. 'Ian, is this——'

'Jordan's wife,' he finished excitedly.

'Oh, I see,' Laura blushed. 'I'm sorry, Kelly, I didn't mean to sound rude just now. I—I——'

'That's all right,' Kelly assured her. I'd probably be jealous too if I had a lovely husband like Ian.'

'But you have. I mean——' Laura blushed again. 'Well, Jordan is—very nice.'

'Yes,' Kelly agreed dully. 'Which reminds me, I have to be getting back. He'll be expecting me.'

'You're back together?—I'm sorry,' Ian instantly apologised, 'that's none of my business. How is your father?'

'Getting better.'

'Is he home now?'

'Oh yes. Today, actually. He's staying with Jordan and me.'

'Could you perhaps get away one evening?' Laura asked, the sharpness now gone from her tone, her naturally sweet nature back in evidence. Kelly could understand such possessiveness, she had once been like that about Jordan. 'Ian and I would love for you and Jordan to come over to dinner.'

'Surely not,' Kelly refused. 'I'm sure you don't want to be

bothered with company now, not when the baby is so near.'

'There's nothing Laura likes more than entertaining,' Ian teased. 'Even now.'

'Well, if you're sure,' she accepted uncertainly. 'I'll have to check with Jordan, of course . . .' she stood up in preparation of leaving.

'I'll call him,' Ian instantly suggested.

Kelly took her leave of them, hurrying out to her car. It wasn't that she didn't like the Smythes, it was that she didn't relish the idea of appearing socially as Jordan's wife. It was bad enough in front of her father, in front of other people it would be ludicrous.

Jordan was pacing up and down the lounge when she let herself into the house. 'Where have you been?' he demanded as soon as he saw her.

Kelly put her handbag down on the sidetable. 'I told you where I was going.'

He swung her round, his face dark with anger. 'I called Maggie, she said she left you hours ago.'

Kelly's eyes widened with indignation. 'You *called* Maggie?'

'Yes,' he bit out.

'My father, is he——'

'He's fine,' Jordan interrupted.

She frowned at him. 'Were you checking up on me, then?'

'Don't be so damned silly,' he dismissed tersely. 'You were late, and I——'

'You were concerned about me!' Kelly derided.

'Yes, damn you, I was! After the way you drove off this afternoon you could have had an accident for all I knew,' he rasped.

'I'm not prone to them. I wasn't driving last time, if that's what you're implying.'

'It wasn't,' he sighed, running a hand through the dark thickness of his hair. 'I know you're usually a sensible driver, but the way you drove off this afternoon wasn't in the least sensible.'

'If you're really interested in why I was late——'

'I am,' he insisted grimly.

She shrugged. 'Then I met an old friend.'

Jordan stiffened, his eyes narrowing suspiciously. 'A friend?'

Kelly nodded. 'Of yours.'

'Mine?' he echoed sharply.

'Yes. Would you like to know who?' she taunted. 'Frightened it might be one of your girl-friends?'

'Kelly!' he said warningly.

'I met Ian and his lovely wife.' She explained the meeting as briefly as she could. 'Ian is going to call you about dinner. I'll leave it up to you whether or not you accept.'

'Do you want to go?'

She shrugged. 'I like Laura, but——'

'Then we'll go,' Jordan decided firmly. 'Your father won't mind just for one evening. I'll arrange it for some time next week.'

'All right. They—They're having a baby.' Kelly looked down at her hands. 'Any day now, I should say.'

'I see.' His mouth was tight.

She looked up, her eyes accusing. 'You notice I said *they* are having a baby, not just that Laura is.'

'I noticed,' Jordan snapped. 'I take it that dig was aimed at me?' He was pacing the room once again.

'You know it was.' She turned as her father entered the room. 'Hello, darling,' she kissed him warmly on the cheek. 'You're looking better after your rest.'

'I feel better. Although you've had Jordan very worried,' he scolded. 'As a brand new husband he's bound to worry if you're later than you said you would be.'

So her father knew about it too! 'I've apologised in a suitable manner,' she gave a teasing smile.

'Have you now?' her father grinned. 'Then maybe I should have knocked before coming in.'

She laughed as she knew she was expected to. 'You have a naughty mind.'

'I remember your mother and I used to do a lot of kissing and cuddling when we were first married. That's how you were born,' he added ruefully.

'Charming!' she gave him a light kiss. 'I'm going up to change for dinner. I won't be long.'

'Didn't you forget to kiss me?' The mocking light in Jordan's eyes challenged her.

She paused at the door. 'I think you've had quite enough for one day.'

'Rationing me already,' he shook his head at her father.

Kelly laughingly left the room, the humour leaving her face as soon as she closed the door behind her. How dared Jordan challenge her like that! She would make her feelings very plain about kissing him as soon as her father had gone to bed.

Jordan was at his most charming through dinner, very attentive towards her, and she knew her father watched them with a satisfied glint in his eye. Well, at least he was happy, and convinced of *their* happiness too.

They all had a game of cards after dinner, Jordan winning as he usually did. When they were first married Jordan had taught her how to play strip poker, demanding an article of her clothing each time she lost. She had always ended up stark naked while he was still fully dressed. And when she had accused him of cheating he had instantly stripped himself. What followed usually made them forget all about playing cards.

'You aren't concentrating, Kelly,' her father interrupted her thoughts.

A guilty look in Jordan's direction showed her that he had guessed her thoughts. Her face coloured as his mouth twisted derisively. 'Sorry, Daddy. I—I think I'm a little tired.'

'I think we all are.' Jordan packed the cards away. 'Time for bed.'

'You could be right.' Kelly's father stretched tiredly. 'I feel as weak as a kitten.'

Jordan stood up, moving to the drinks cabinet. 'Care for a nightcap?' He held up the whisky decanter.

'Thanks,' her father accepted.

'Not for me,' Kelly said wearily. 'I'm for bed. Goodnight.' She moved to the door.

'Doesn't a father merit a goodnight kiss now that you have a husband?' her father teased.

'Of course.' She smilingly kissed him on the cheek, the look she slanted at Jordan daring him to ask for one too. He didn't, his mocking smile acknowledgement of her challenge.

The bedclothes were turned back invitingly and her lacy nightgown lay across the bed. So much was like it used to be, except that tonight this huge double bed would hold only her. She shouldn't find that so strange—hadn't she slept alone here for two months before her separation from Jordan?

She heard her father going to his room as she left the shower, wrapping a towel about herself as she entered the bedroom. Jordan was there, pulling his tie loose from his throat, the jacket to his suit already hanging in the wardrobe.

'Wh-what are you doing here?' she gasped.

He gave her a pitying glance. 'Getting ready for bed. I would have thought that was obvious.'

Kelly stood firm, her mouth set stubbornly. 'You aren't sleeping in here!'

'Try and stop me.' Jordan's stance became challenging, his feet set slightly apart, his arms folded across the broadness of his chest.

CHAPTER FIVE

'I INTEND to.' Her eyes sparkled angrily. 'I may have to share this house with you, but I have no intention of sharing the bedroom too. Use the room you used to sleep in, that shouldn't be any hardship to you.'

'Your father is in that room.'

'Then use one of the others,' Kelly said shrilly, clinging to the towel as if her life depended on it. 'Goodness knows there are enough of them.'

'I'm staying right here. Your father will expect it.'

'My father?' Kelly looked startled. 'But he won't know where you sleep!'

'And if he should need anything in the night? If he should wake up early in the morning and come knocking on our door?'

'He won't.' But she sounded less certain, Jordan noting her hesitation by the triumphant gleam in his eyes. 'If you won't sleep somewhere else, Jordan, then I will!' She marched over to the door.

'I think not, Kelly,' his hand came out and gripped her upper arm. 'I think we should settle this thing here and now.'

She looked up at him with apprehensive eyes, aware of her vulnerability clothed only in a bathtowel. 'Settle what here and now?' she asked breathlessly, fascinated by the pulse beating in his throat.

Jordan's breathing was shallow, a taut control to the sensuousness of his lips. 'I think you know what,' he told her softly, his eyes intent on her face.

Her head went back, her gaze meeting his unflinchingly. 'I have no idea what you're talking about.'

'No?' Jordan taunted. 'Oh, I think you have.'

'I haven't!' She tried to remove his fingers from her arm, but all that did was entice him to increase the pressure. 'You're hurting me!' she choked, hating having to show him any sign of weakness.

'Yes,' he acknowledged huskily. 'I can't seem to do anything else. But I'd like to! Do you remember how it was with us, Kelly? Do you remember——'

'I remember nothing!' she cut in, instantly stopping the caressing movement of his thumb on her arm. 'I haven't thought about you in years, so why should I be able to remember what it was like being married to you?' The defiance in her voice was echoed in her flashing eyes.

Jordan's mouth was a thin angry line, the pulse in his throat beating even faster. 'Then maybe I should refresh your memory for you,' he said tautly.

'No!' Kelly's head jerked sideways as he began to lower his mouth towards hers.

'Yes, Kelly!' His hands came up to hold her head immobile and his lips claimed hers. He moved his mouth slowly against her, the tension in his body building by the second. 'Oh yes, Kelly,' he groaned agonisingly, pulling her against the hard length of his body before his mouth again claimed hers. 'Think of me now, Kelly, think of me now and want me,' he encouraged huskily.

She couldn't believe this was happening to her, couldn't believe this dizzy sensation, the way she swayed towards Jordan of her own volition, entwining her arms about his neck, her mouth raised invitingly.

'You do want me!' he cried in disbelief.

'No. I——'

'Yes, you do!' he shouted his triumph, swinging her up in his arms, the bathtowel slipping precariously.

As he laid her on the bed Kelly didn't resist the complete removal of the towel, lying before him like a golden

Aphrodite, her breasts pert and in iting, her stomach smooth and flat, her thighs silky soft. Jordan's eyes darkened to black as he hurriedly removed his own clothes, his gaze never leaving her, his desire a tangible thing.

'My God, you're beautiful,' he groaned as he joined her on the bed, kissing her, starting with her throat and slowly going downwards.

Jordan was beautiful too; she had forgotten just how beautiful. His shoulders were wide and powerful, his chest liberally sprinkled with silky hair, his stomach taut and firm, his thighs strong and sure. Kelly's hands smoothed over his muscular shoulders, loving the feel of his firm flesh beneath her fingertips.

She gasped as his lips claimed the tautness of one nipple, his tongue moving caressingly over the fiery tip. The darkness of his head against her creamy skin was a familiar scene, enticingly so.

Desire ran through her veins like liquid fire, her legs entwining with the muscular roughness of his, a heady excitement making her feel dizzy. For too long she had been denied Jordan's possession, the mindless pleasure he always gave her when they made love, and she moved against him restlessly, impatient for his full lovemaking.

'Kelly?' he raised his head questioningly. 'You know I have to take you, don't you?'

'Yes,' she nodded, her voice breathless. Yes, she knew Jordan was out of control, had known it since he had first kissed her.

'Don't try to stop me,' his lips plundered the hollows of her throat. 'For God's sake don't stop me, Kelly!' he groaned hungrily.

She didn't, offering no resistance as his thighs came between hers, raising her hips to meet the hard demand of his body. She cried out as he took her, the initial possession as painful to her as it had been on their wedding night; her body had grown unaccustomed to the fierceness of Jordan's.

'Oh God!' he shuddered at her pain. 'I'm sorry, darling, so sorry. But I can't stop now—I can't!'

She didn't want him to; the pain faded and wild desire flooded back. Her movements matched his own the climax to their heated senses reached as one, shuddering back to earth in each other's arms.

Jordan's expression was agonised as he looked down at her. 'What have I done?' He rolled away from her, his eyes closed as if to shut out the sight of her. 'My God, what have I done?' he groaned again.

A sudden chill washed over Kelly as she asked herself the same question. What had *she* done? Jordan couldn't be blamed for what had just happened, men were only made to be pushed so far. It had been up to her to say no, she had no doubt that Jordan would have accepted her refusal. But now it was too late, too late for him to feel anything else but contempt for the easy way she had fallen victim to her own desire. How he must despise her now that his body had received its full satisfaction, now that he was able to think rationally once again.

She watched him as he stood up to pull on his towelling robe, lighting up a cheroot with shaking fingers. He put up a hand to his temple, massaging there, as if his head ached. 'I didn't mean that to happen,' he said raggedly. 'What I'm trying to say is——'

'That it was a mistake,' Kelly finished dully, the top sheet pulled over her to hide her nakedness.

Jordan gave her a sharp look. 'Not exactly,' he sighed.

'But it was,' she insisted calmly. 'A mistake that would be better forgotten by both of us.'

He drew hard on the cheroot held between long tapered fingers. 'You think I can forget that?' he asked harshly, a white ring of tension about his mouth. 'Just act as if it never happened?'

Kelly shrugged with a casualness she was far from feeling. 'You could try,' she dismissed. 'Just chalk it down as yet another woman in your bed.'

His eyes were icy grey. 'But you're my wife!'

A bitter smile curved her lips. 'What a novel experience for you.'

'Kelly——'

'Would you mind if I went to sleep now?' she interrupted him, the strain of acting normally beginning to tell on her. 'I'm feeling rather tired.'

Jordan stubbed out his half-smoked cheroot with savage movements, moving to grasp her shoulders, shaking her angrily. 'You can't go to sleep after what just happened,' he told her fiercely.

'What else would you suggest I do?'

His eyes darkened in colour. 'You really want to know?' he asked throatily.

It was happening again, to both of them. A slight flush appeared beneath Jordan's pale skin, his hands tightening compulsively on her arms, his breathing once again becoming shallow. And Kelly could feel her bones melting, could feel herself moving towards Jordan even though she tried not to.

'This time,' Jordan told her slowly, his gaze fixed on her moist, parted lips. 'This time,' he repeated, once more on the bed beside her, 'there will be no mistake about it, for either of us,' he added harshly.

Their movements were slow and leisurely, each knowing exactly how to please the other, in no hurry to bring their caresses to their tumultuous climax. The first time they had been hungry for satisfaction, this time each caress took a lifetime, each kiss more druggingly intimate than the last.

Then once again their emotions were spiralling out of control, their pleasure exploding into a thousand coloured lights. Jordan collapsed against her breasts, his arms holding her tightly to him, his even breathing soon telling her that he had fallen asleep.

Kelly had no idea where all this would end; she didn't want to look beyond this moment. She would live life as it came, take each day, and night, as they came.

She was awake early the next morning, Jordan still fast asleep against her breasts. His arms tightened about her as she tried to slip out of bed, and she lay still, waiting until he had settled into sleep once again before moving away from him. This time he made no effort to stop her. Kelly moved quietly about the room collecting her clothes for the day before going into the bathroom.

She deliberately didn't think of last night's events, shutting her mind off from all soul-searching, sticking to her decision not to delve into the whys and wherefores of last night. She was married to Jordan. Okay, so they no longer lived together, but they were still man and wife, and there was nothing wrong with what had happened between them during the night.

'Breakfast, Mrs Lord?' Mrs McLeod came into the lounge where Kelly was searching for her handbag.

She turned to smile at the housekeeper. 'Not for me, thank you. But I think my husband might appreciate a cup of coffee in bed before he goes to work.'

'Very well, Mrs Lord,' the other woman beamed.

'I'm going out myself, Mrs McLeod.' Kelly at last found her handbag, taking out her purse and car keys. 'My father should be asleep for some time.'

'Can I expect you back for lunch?' the housekeeper enquired politely.

'Oh yes,' Kelly didn't hesitate to confirm this, 'I'm only going for a short drive.'

'It's so nice to have you all back here,' Mrs McLeod told her shyly.

'It's nice to be here,' Kelly smiled. 'I should be back

before my father comes down.'

She didn't even know where she was going, she just wanted to get herself together before she had to face Jordan again. It was cowardly of her, and no doubt he would have something to say about it when next they met, but for the moment she wanted to cherish the thought of last night to herself.

In Jordan's arms she had come alive again, left behind her the cool facade she had adopted the last five years. And before she saw Jordan she was going to have to regain some of that coolness. He had made love to her, been as out of control as she was, and yet except for their mutual groans of pleasure neither of them had spoken a work.

There had been no words spoken between them, and no love shown. But Kelly did love him, that much she now knew. Whatever had happened to her five years ago had only numbed her feelings, being with Jordan had shown her that her love for him was still very much alive.

The trouble was how was she going to hide it from him. She couldn't be put through the humiliating experience of Jordan knowing, wouldn't let him destroy her with her own love a second time.

The drive out had cleared her head, put her thoughts in some order. She would take what affection Jordan cared to give, would accept his kisses, but she wouldn't let him know the true state of her feelings. She wouldn't fall into that trap again.

Her father was in the lounge when she arrived back at the house. He looked up as she entered the room. 'You've missed Jordan by minutes.' He stood up to kiss her on the cheek.

She hadn't missed him at all, she had passed him on the road, and although he had signalled for her to stop she had merely acknowledged him with a wave of her hand. Her cloying, loving attitude had bored him so much before that he had turned to another woman only weeks after their wedding; this time he would find her coolly sophisticated. Maybe that way she would be able to get him back on a permanent basis, be able to hold his interest for longer than a few weeks.

She smiled at her father. 'I'll see him later. What shall we do today?'

He shrugged. 'What do you suggest?'

'How about a drive to the coast? We could laze on the beach, go for a swim. You could even buy me some candyfloss,' she added with a grin.

'That's a deal. But breakfast first, hmm?'

'Lovely,' Kelly eagerly agreed. 'I'm starving!'

In the end they both ate a hearty breakfast, laughing together as they collected their things for the beach.

It was almost lunchtime by the time they reached Brighton, one of the nearest coastal resorts to London.

'How do you fancy going to the nudist beach?' Kelly teased her father once they had changed into their costumes.

He frowned. 'Nudist beach?'

Kelly bit her lip. Her first day alone with her father and already she had forgotten his loss of memory. The nudist beach had only been open a year or so, and so her father couldn't possibly know of its existence.

She gave a light, casual laugh, putting her arm through the crook of his. 'Didn't you hear about it? It's still in the experimental stage, just to see if anyone wants to use it.'

'Well, I don't,' he instantly refused. 'Although I wouldn't mind strolling along there to take a look.' There was a wicked glint in his eyes.

Kelly laughed. 'You and a couple of hundred others!'

'I suppose so,' he agreed ruefully. 'Okay, I'll race you into the sea.'

Kelly grimaced. 'Over these stones that pass as the beach you won't race me anywhere. Where's the sand?'

'Under the stones?' he suggested hopefully, grinning widely.

The sea was icy cold, and they spent only a short time in its chilling depths, coming out on to the pebbly beach to towel themselves dry.

'How about lunch?' Kelly asked with a shiver.

'Fine. Where do you want to eat?'

'Right here,' she grinned. 'You lay out the towels, I'll go and get the fish and chips.'

'I'm sure your menu was a bit more refined in Barbados,' her father laughed.

Kelly flushed, at least remembering she was just supposed to have come back from there. 'It may have been more refined,' she teased. 'But it was certainly no more enjoyable. Give me ten minutes and then send out the search-party.' She pulled her denims on over the bottom of her bikini. 'I'll be over at the nudist beach if you can't find me.'

'If you go I go!' he warned.

She was back within minutes, watching with enjoyment the unusual sight of her father eating fish and chips out of a newspaper. An exclusive restaurant was more his venue, although he seemed to enjoy the food she had bought him.

'No dessert?' he teased her as they disposed of the vinegar-soaked newspaper.

'No. But I bought us these instead.' She produced two cans of Coca-Cola from her handbag.

'You really know how to provide a stylish lunch!' he drank thirstily.

'Go on, you know you loved it,' Kelly laughed, lying back on her towel, and quickly fell asleep in the sunshine.

'You've been sleeping like a baby,' her father told her when she woke up. 'Jordan keeping you awake nights, is he?' He chuckled as she blushed fiery red.

He was so near the truth that she couldn't help her blushes. She had been so tired just now that she had fallen into an exhausted sleep.

'Just for that,' she stood up, 'you can buy me that candyfloss after all!'

They both had one in the end, Kelly laughing uproariously as her father got it all over him.

'It's all right for you to laugh!' he untangled himself from the sticky confection. 'As I'm a lot older than you it's a damned sight longer since I had any of this stuff, and I know everyone says this, but it isn't as good as it was when I was young. And talking of ages——'

'Yes?' Her voice was sharp, sure that he had realised she no longer looked like a naïve eighteen-year-old. In fact, she was surprised he hadn't mentioned it before.

'I keep getting funny looks from people.' He disgustedly disposed of the candyfloss in the nearest litter-bin. 'I'm sure they think I'm your aged boy-friend.'

Kelly had noticed a couple of curious looks in their direction, but she hadn't realised their reason. She grinned at her father. 'Let's really give them something to look at!' She stood on tiptoe and kissed him, putting her hand through the crook of his arm. 'How does it feel to be thought a dirty old man?'

'Quite good, actually,' he laughed. 'Quite a boost for my ego.' He suddenly became serious. 'Marriage seems to agree with you.'

Her smile became forced. 'Did you think it wouldn't?' she asked lightly.

'I wasn't sure,' he shrugged. 'Knowing how Jordan feels about you——'

'He told you about that?' she interrupted sharply.

'He and I had a chat when he asked you to marry him. Why do you think I tried to make you wait a while? I knew that it wouldn't be easy living with a man who feels about you the way Jordan does.'

It seemed that at least Jordan had admitted to her

father that his sole interest in her was physical. 'If you knew how he felt why did you let me marry him?' she wanted to know. 'Surely you must have realised how difficult I find it to accept these feelings.'

'I thought you could cope with it. Besides, you wanted to marry him.'

'Yes,' she agreed dully. 'Yes, I did.'

'Aren't you happy, Kelly?' he asked anxiously.

No stress or strain, she must remember that. 'You must know I am,' she gave a glowing smile. 'We both are.'

'It's difficult to tell. On the surface Jordan is such an unemotional man.'

It wasn't only on the surface. Except for the natural sexual urges Jordan funtioned as a machine. 'We're happy. Now stop worrying needlessly.' She looked at her wrist-watch. 'I think we should be getting back now, we don't want to be late for dinner.'

Her father quirked one eyebrow. 'No quick look at the nudist beach?'

'In your state of health?' she grinned. 'Certainly not!'

'Spoilsport!' he moaned.

It was almost seven by the time they got back, and Kelly half expected Jordan to be pacing the hallway as he had been yesterday. She felt a sense of disappointment when he wasn't. He wasn't in the lounge either, or the bedroom when she looked there.

'Mrs McLeod,' she went down to the kitchen, 'is my husband home yet?'

'No, Mrs Lord.' The housekeeper was in the middle of helping cook prepare dinner. 'He rang earlier to say he'd been delayed.'

Kelly felt a familiar sinking sensation in her stomach. 'Oh!'

'He said that a business meeting had come up unexpectedly.'

'I see.' Kelly bit her lip. It was such a familiar story, painfully so. 'Did he give any indication of when he would be home? If it isn't too late perhaps we could delay dinner for him.'

'Mr Lord said not to wait dinner, that he could be quite late.'

'Thank you,' she accepted jerkily, her hands twisting nervously together. 'Serve dinner at the usual time, then, Mrs McLeod.'

She turned on her heel and left the kitchen, going up to her bedroom. The double bed in there seemed to mock her. Only hours ago she and Jordan had shared that bed, and now he was making up the usual excuse to see one of his women. Well, he wouldn't see her depressed and miserable as she used to be when he called to say he would be late. Tonight when he got home he would find her either already asleep or coolly polite, depending on how late it actually was when he got here.

'No Jordan?' her father seemed surprised by his absence.

'Business,' Kelly dismissed tersely. 'So perhaps you would like to do the honours and pour the drinks?'

He poured her a sherry and a whisky for himself. 'Talking of business, I shall have to get back to work soon. There's nothing wrong with me now, and I feel such a fraud lazing about here.'

'There's no hurry,' she said smoothly. 'Miles can cope admirably.' Thank goodness her father had had the same assistant for the last twenty years! 'A short holiday won't do you any harm.'

'But I was in the middle of buying out Landers,' he complained.

Landers was a retail company her father had bought out years ago. In fact, it brought him quite a nice yearly profit nowadays. 'Miles is just as capable of dealing with it,' she insisted. 'And the doctor told you're not to even attempt to go back to work just yet.'

'It surely wouldn't hurt for me just to go in one morning or afternoon? I could just check to make sure Miles is handling everything the way I would myself.'

They went in to dinner, and Mrs McLeod served them the first course. 'Miles handles everything the way you would,' Kelly teased lightly. 'He always has done.'

'But——'

'I really don't think it's a good idea,' Kelly said firmly. 'I know you, Daddy, it wouldn't stop at Landers. I have a better idea. How about if Miles brings the work here? That way we can be sure you don't get involved too much.' They could also vet any work that he saw! She knew her father well enough to believe he wouldn't just accept his inactivity. If they didn't let him work here then he would merely find a way of getting to the office without them knowing about it. 'What do you think?' she asked him.

'I'd rather go to the office——'

'That's definitely out. You either work here or nothing. I mean it, Daddy. The doctor only let you leave hospital at all because you promised to take things easy. Jordan and I could easily see that you're readmitted,' she threatened at his stubborn expression.

'All right,' he finally accepted with a sigh. 'But I'll get Miles out here first thing in the morning.'

'Afternoon,' Kelly insisted. 'You had a hectic day today, I think you should rest in the morning.'

'You're very bossy all of a sudden,' he scowled.

'That comes of being your daughter and Jordan's wife,' she said cheekily.

Her father laughed at her unrelenting attitude. 'I guess it does at that. Okay, afternoon. Do you order Jordan about like this too?'

Kelly quirked an eyebrow. 'What do you think?'

'I think no.'

She grinned. 'Right.'

They listened to records after dinner, although after an hour or so Kelly could see her father's eyes beginning to droop tiredly. She tactfully suggested they both have an early night, knowing he would refuse point blank if the suggestion was made only to him. Not that she had any intention of going to sleep herself, it was only ten o'clock, but she could always have a read in bed.

She heard the car in the driveway just before eleven o'clock. Even for Jordan this was exceptionally late, and her mouth set angrily, although she quickly dampened this down as she heard Jordan's firm tread on the stairs. He seemed to hesitate for a second or two before opening the bedroom door, his sharp gaze instantly swinging in Kelly's direction as she lay in the bed making a show of reading a magazine.

Kelly studied him beneath lowered lashes, noting how well the dark grey suit fitted across his wide shoulders, how the cut of his trousers emphasised the powerful length of his thighs. His tie was loosened at his throat, the top two buttons of his shirt undone. He looked lean and attractive, ruggedly so.

He eyed Kelly warily as he closed the door behind him. 'Did you have a nice day?'

'Yes, thank you. Daddy and I went to the coast.' She put her magazine to one side, giving him her full attention.

Jordan nodded. 'So Mrs McLeod informed me. Brighton, wasn't it?'

'Mm.' Jordan was uncertain of her mood, she could see that. Well, he was in for a shock if he thought she was going to cause any sort of scene, about last night or this evening. Play it cool, she had decided, and she was going to keep to that. She gave him a bright smile. 'We ate fish and chips out of newspaper and then covered ourselves in candyfloss,' she told him.

'I bet your father loved that,' he said dryly.

'Strangely enough he did. He was quite relaxed by the time we got home. Although he's decided he wants to see Miles.' Kelly went on to tell him of her suggestion, seeing his puzzlement about her calm behaviour increasing by the minute. 'I couldn't think what else to do,' she added.

'It's a good idea, I wish I'd thought of it.' He ran his hand through the dark thickness of his hair, an air of weariness to his movements.

'Did you have a bad day?' she asked softly.

Jordan's gaze sharpened, although he met only polite query on her face. 'Well, it wasn't good,' he said heavily.

'Why don't you go and have a shower, and then I'll massage your neck like I used to,' Kelly offered. 'You always said that relaxed you,' she added with feigned innocence. Her caressing movements on his neck and back had relaxed him—before he made love to her! She could see Jordan's puzzlement growing.

He frowned darkly. 'Kelly, yesterday I asked you to come back to me. Are you now offering to do just that?' His eyes were narrowed.

'I'm *offering* to massage your neck,' she shrugged. 'But if you don't want me to . . .' She snuggled down under the covers as if going to sleep, yawning tiredly for good measure.

'Oh, I want you to,' Jordan told her hurriedly. 'I'll be two minutes, don't go to sleep.'

'I'll try not to,' she yawned again.

He must have broken all records showering. He was back within the two minutes, a towel wrapped about his waist, his hair slighly damp. Kelly had to hide a smile at the eagerness with which he lay face down on the bed. Her cool, calm attitude seemed to be working—even if she was a burning mass of jealousy inside. But none of that showed in her serene expression, and that was the way it was going to stay.

'Mm,' he groaned as her fingertips ran lightly down his spine. 'You always did have the most sensuous hands I've ever known.'

Kelly loved touching him like this, had always enjoyed these nightly rituals as much as he had. His skin was smooth and brown, firmly muscled, and she could feel the tension leaving him with each stroke of her fingertips. He lay with his eyes closed, his head resting on his arms, a look of utter contentment on his face.

'You like?' Kelly asked huskily, feeling the excitement coursing through her, a tingling sensation going up through her hands and down her body. And Jordan wasn't unaffected, she could tell that by the high flush to his cheeks, his ragged breathing.

'I more than like,' he confirmed. 'I'm sorry about this evening, Kelly. Normanson flew in from New York and I had to meet with him. You remember Normanson?'

She did, vaguely. They had had him to dinner a couple of times. He was a business friend of Jordan's. 'Yes, I remember him.' She massaged his nape, registering his moans of pleasure.

'I would have got out of it if I could,' Jordan murmured.

'It didn't matter.' Her hands were on his shoulders now. 'Daddy and I were all right, and you have to do your work.' She continued her caressing movements.

'Yes,' he sighed. 'But after last night——'

'Last night?' Kelly repeated sharply, her cool momentarily deserting her.

She got herself together with effort. 'What was so special about last night?' she asked lightly.

He rolled over, more dangerous in this position, his gaze unashamedly lingering on the scantiness of her pale green silky nightgown, her breasts firm and uptilted be-

neath the revealing material. 'You ask me that?' he said
huskily soft, his hands firm on her upper arms.

'Yes,' she smiled. 'We're married, Jordan. We're perfectly entitled to last night.'

'But you aren't coming back to me?' His eyes were
narrowed to icy grey slits.

'I couldn't make a decision like that on the basis of one
night together,' she shrugged.

'Kelly?' he frowned. 'What are you suggesting? That
we carry on like this, sleeping together and yet making no
commitment to each other?'

She sat back on her heels. Yes, that was exactly what
she was suggesting, until he could make her the kind of
commitment she wanted, and that was total.

She gave a casual shrug. 'I'm not ready to make a
commitment to anyone.' She watched him as he swung
off the bed, standing up to discard the towel and pull on
his bathrobe. 'Where are you going?' she asked as he
moved to the door.

The look he gave her was savage, his eyes blazing, his
mouth taut. 'To get a drink,' he snapped.

'Like that?' she indicated his state of undress.

'Stark naked if I feel like it!' he told her harshly.

Kelly shrugged. 'Shall I wait for you?'

'No,' he said grimly, slamming the door after him.

Kelly took him at his word and didn't stay awake for
him, turning off all the lights except the lamp on Jordan's
side of the bed and snuggling down under the blankets.
She hoped Jordan didn't drink too much, his temper was
foul when he had a hangover.

He couldn't have drunk much at all, he had only been
gone five minutes. Kelly turned over to look at him, blinking to wake herself from the light doze she had drifted into.

His savagery hadn't left him as he came to sit on the
side of the bed, lifting her roughly towards him. 'I want

you,' he ground out fiercely. '*Want* you!' he repeated with a groan.

Kelly faced him unflinchingly. 'I'm not saying no, Jordan,' she told him softly.

'Then why the hell aren't you?' He shook her hard. 'I can't believe this is you talking. You don't love me, you aren't willing to become my wife again, and yet you want to go to bed with me.'

'You're a good lover, Jordan. I've missed sleeping with you.'

His eyes turned black. 'And I've missed sleeping with you!' he said raggedly. 'Come here,' he demanded.

She wasn't resisting. There was no gentleness in him as he possessed her, only hard demand and mind-shattering sensations. Wave after wave of pleasure washed over her, leaving her weak and clinging to him. If anything their lovemaking had been better than last night.

'Have there been any other lovers for you, Kelly?' Jordan asked her as he lit up a cheroot.

'No.' She wasn't going to lie about something as important as that, not even if she did think it would make him jealous.

'Why haven't there?' He watched her through a haze of smoke.

She shrugged. 'I've been kept busy travelling with my father.'

'In other words you just didn't have the time for lovers,' he said dryly.

Or the inclination. After Jordan she hadn't believed herself capable of feeling attracted to any man. And yet she could feel, for Jordan, only for Jordan. 'Something like that,' she agreed huskily.

'And now you have the time,' he said bitterly.

'Yes.'

Jordan ground out the cheroot in the onyx ashtray on

his side-table. 'Then I'd better make sure you don't waste a moment of it!' His mouth came down viciously on hers, his thighs once more hardening with desire.

Kelly was woken the next morning by a loud hammering noise, and emerged from under the bedclothes to realise that someone was banging on the bedroom door. Jordan was already out of bed, just tying the belt of his bathrobe.

'What is it?' Kelly blinked dazedly. 'What's wrong?'

'I have no idea,' he snapped, moving towards the door. 'But I mean to find out.' He flung the door open. 'Mrs McLeod,' he frowned. 'What is it?'

'Oh, sir, sir!' she was obviously very agitated. 'I had no way of knowing, Mr Lord. I hadn't read the newspapers myself, you see.'

'Mrs McLeod,' Jordan interrupted firmly, 'you aren't making much sense.'

'No, I'm not, am I?' She sighed. 'Here,' she held out a newspaper, 'this should explain it all.'

He took the newspaper from her. 'Oh, hell!' he groaned, looking up. 'Mr Darrow has seen this?'

'Yes, sir. That's why I——'

'All right, Mrs McLeod,' he said firmly, 'I'll deal with this now. Mr Darrow is still in his room?'

'Yes, Mr Lord. And he's very upset. He——'

'What is it?' Kelly got out of bed to join them. 'Jordan?'

He handed her the newspaper. Kelly looked down at it. The headlines read, 'Businessman David Darrow loses memory after accident'.

CHAPTER SIX

'How did this happen?' Kelly gasped.

'The how of it can be discussed at some other time.' Jordan's tone was grim. 'You call Dr Jones and have him get over here, and I'll go and calm your father down.'

'Yes, yes, of course. I—I'll do that.'

The doctor agreed to come over immediately, promising to be there within ten minutes. Kelly hurriedly dressed in navy blue trousers and light blue blouse before going to her father's bedroom.

'I had a right to be told!' her father could be heard shouting. 'I'm not a child to be pampered and humoured!'

'Calm down, David,' Jordan soothed. 'I'm well aware of the fact that you aren't a child——'

'Then why the hell keep something like this from me?'

'David——'

'Daddy,' Kelly went into the room. Her father looked completely harasssed, his skin white beneath the tan. 'We only did it for the best. The doctors——'

'Yes, the doctors!' he stormed. 'What on earth were they thinking of not telling me I've forgotten five years of my life? My God, do you realise I'm fifty-one and not forty-six as I thought I was? What the hell are you smiling about?' he turned on Kelly. 'It isn't funny,' he complained angrily.

'You are,' she contradicted. 'All you're worried about is the fact that you're older than you thought you were.'

A reluctant smile lightened his features. 'It's all right for you, you're only twenty-three, I'm *fifty-one*!'

Kelly was relieved to see that some of the tension had now left him, that this moment of humour had relaxed him somewhat. Nevertheless, she felt glad when the doctor was shown into the bedroom, asking to be alone with his patient.

Jordan moved about their own bedroom, dressing in brown fitted trousers and shirt. 'How did it get into the papers?' he said impatiently, lighting up a cheroot to pace the room.

Kelly sat down on the bed. 'I have no idea.'

'No one else knew but us, and some of the hospital staff, of, course.'

'I doubt it was one of them.'

Jordan picked up the newspaper in which the story was featured. 'Ben Durston,' he read out the reporter's name. 'I've never heard of him. Have you?'

Anger flared in her violet eyes. 'Are you implying——'

'I'm not implying anything,' he sighed. 'I'm just trying to find out where he got his information. Somehow this man, Ben Durston, found out about your father. I want to know how.'

'Well, it wasn't me,' Kelly snapped.

'And it wasn't from me. So it must have been someone at the hospital, one of the nurses perhaps.' He took a cream jacket out of the wardrobe and slipped in on over his powerful shoulders.

'Where are you going?' Kelly wanted to know.

'To see Ben Durston,' Jordan scowled. 'I want to know who his source was. Luckily enough it seems your father is taking it very well. He's a little shocked right now, but he'll get over it. Maybe it would have been better if he had been told the truth from the start.'

'Perhaps,' she agreed. 'But Dr Jones said, and we agreed with him at the time, that to tell him might be more harmful.'

'Maybe, but he's good and mad about it now. I'll be back later.' Jordan straightened his cuff.

'Aren't you going in to work today?'

'No,' he said curtly.

'Poor Janet, she will be disappointed.'

'Kelly!'

She gave him a sweet smile. 'Forgive me, Jordan, I forgot this ability you have to satisfy more than one woman at the same time.'

'Not simultaneously, I hope?' his mouth twisted mockingly.

Kelly's expression hardened. 'Will you be back in time for lunch?'

'That depends on how long it takes to get the information I want.'

Knowing how persuasive he could be she didn't think he would be late back. Jordan was one of those people who liked to get his own way—and he usually succeeded. 'I'll tell Mrs McLeod you'll be here for lunch, then,' she told him coolly.

'Will you be here?'

She shrugged. 'I'm not sure——'

'Kelly, we have to talk——'

'I don't know what about,' her voice was brittlely light.

'Last night——'

'Oh, not that again, Jordan,' she cut in impatiently. 'Did you enjoy last night?'

Dark colour flooded his cheeks. 'You know I did,' he revealed tightly.

'And so did I. Now let's stop making a federal case out of it.'

'But, Kelly, we can't just—just keep sleeping together!' he said in exasperation.

'Why can't we? We're married.'

His face darkened angrily. 'God, I can't talk to you when you're in this mood.'

'Then don't even try.' She stood up to begin straightening the bed. 'Shouldn't you be going?' She gave him a pointed glance.

'I'll deal with you later,' he told her grimly.

Kelly gave him an enticing smile. 'I'll look forward to it.'

He shook his head. 'I'm not sure I know you any more.'

'I don't think you ever knew me, Jordan. You never took the time to do that, you never *had* the time.'

'Well, I'm making time now.'

'That sounded like a threat.'

'More a declaration of intent.' The door closed quietly behind him as he left.

Kelly went back to her father's bedroom, finding him lying on the bed while the doctor examined him. She smiled reassuringly as he glanced her way.

'Well, Doctor?' she asked as he stepped back, closing up his medical bag with a snap.

Michael Jones shrugged. 'Slight shock, but otherwise he's sound.'

'How nice.' Her father swung his legs to the floor. 'I find out it's five years later than I thought it was and I only have slight shock. Great!' he groaned sarcastically.

'You can lie back on that bed,' the doctor told him firmly. 'I said a slight shock, but it was enough for me to want you to have complete rest for today. A light lunch, and then a long sleep. I'll leave you some tablets to help with the sleep.'

'If you think I'm going to calmly lie back here and go to sleep then you're mistaken,' Kelly's father scorned. 'I'm going out, I want to catch up on the last five years of my life.'

'I'm sorry, Mr Darrow, but you aren't going anywhere.

If you won't rest here then I'll have to admit you for a couple of days.' The doctor quirked an eyebrow. 'Which is it to be?'

Kelly watched the stubborn anger in her father's face, expecting the explosion at any moment. To her surprise he lay back weakly against the pillows, a look of weariness on his features.

'I'll stay here,' he accepted ruefully.

'And you'll follow instructions,' the doctor ordered. 'If you don't your daughter has strict instructions to call me.'

Her father glowered at her. 'She would too!'

Kelly and the doctor laughed as they went downstairs together. 'I meant it about the rest,' he told her as they reached the front door. 'Right now your father is feeling angry, when it fully hits him that all that time is a blank then he's going to panic. It would be better if he slept through the worst of that.'

'Jordan and I will make sure he does as he's told,' she assured him.

'That won't be easy,' the doctor sympathised. 'He isn't very good at it.'

'You noticed!' Kelly laughed.

'Yes,' he smiled. 'If he seems any worse give me a call. But I'll be here tomorrow in any case. Now that he knows there's always the possibility that snatches of the past could come to him, unconnected flashes of memory that will finally make up the whole.'

And when that happened she and Jordan would no longer have a need to continue living together! But she mustn't think that way, mustn't be selfish. It was important that her father regain his memory, and she would do all she could to help him do just that.

'In no way try to force the issue,' the doctor instantly disabused her of that idea. 'Only time will help him. Is your husband here?'

'He had to go out. He should be back soon. Did you want to see him?'

'No, not particularly. I just wondered if he had any idea how the story came to be in the newspapers.'

'I think he's just gone to find out,' Kelly smiled at the understatement of that remark.

'I see.' The doctor obviously got the inflection behind it too. 'Oh well, no great harm done. Although it was obviously an irresponsible thing for anyone to do. The shock of that disclosure could have had serious consequences.'

Her father had taken it very well, in fact he was quite jovial during the snack lunch they had together. They ate lunch out in the garden, the sun and fresh air giving her father a colour that had otherwise been lacking. Jordan hadn't yet returned, and Kelly tried hard not to think of reasons why he hadn't.

'Nap, now,' Kelly said firmly, standing up. 'Come on, Daddy—inside!'

He lay on the lounger next to her. 'Couldn't I just stay here and doze off for an hour?'

'An afternoon's sleep, the doctor said,' Kelly insisted, 'and that's what you're going to have.'

'Do I have to?' he groaned.

'You have to.' She held out her hands and pulled him to his feet. 'And you can take two of the tablets the doctor gave me for you.'

'You know I don't like taking tablets,' he grumbled as they entered the lounge. 'Not for anything.'

Kelly poured him some water from the jug on the table, handing him the glass and the two tablets. 'Take them,' she ordered.

'All five years has done for you is make you bossy,' he scowled, swallowing the tablets down.

She laughed. 'It's done more than that, Daddy!'

'I hope I'm not in for too many shocks,' he muttered as they walked up the stairs together.

Kelly sobered. 'Not too many,' she said guardedly.

'I hope not. It's not good for a man of my age.'

Her smile returned. 'I never realised how vain you are,' she chuckled.

He looked affronted. 'I always thought fifty was a milestone I didn't want to reach.'

'I can assure you you met it with great dignity.' She pulled the coverlet over him as he lay down. 'We even had a party,' she remembered fondly.

'Here?' he asked sleepily.

'No, of course—No,' she blushed as she realised she had been about to make another slip-up. She really wasn't very good at this pretence. 'We were in France.'

'Oh, you and Jordan joined me there,' he nodded understanding.

She had no idea where Jordan had been on her father's fiftieth birthday. They had received a congratulations telegram from him, but Kelly couldn't remember where from now.

'Can I get you anything before I go?' She made no further reference to the party, moving to pull the curtains against the bright sunshine.

'No, I'll be fine.' His voice was distinctly slurred now, his eyes closing sleepily.

She bent to gently kiss his forehead. 'Sleep well. I'll see you soon.'

There was still no sign of Jordan when she got downstairs, so she fumed silently to herself out in the garden. He could have at least telephoned to say he had been delayed! Or maybe he couldn't give the reason for his delay, maybe there had been a beautiful blonde at the newspaper office who had attracted his attention. Him and his damned blondes! If he——

'Telephone, Mrs Lord!' Mrs McLeod called from the house.

At last! He must have got her anger by telepathy. 'Yes?' she snapped into the receiver.

'Hey,' drawled a familiar *female* voice, 'I know I had to leave a bit abruptly the other day,' Maggie said lightly. 'But I didn't expect that sort of reaction when next we spoke.'

The tension left her in a sigh. 'Sorry, Maggie. That anger wasn't meant for you.'

'Jordan?' Maggie guessed dryly.

'Who else?'

'Quite,' Maggie agreed. 'By that I take it he isn't there?'

'No.'

'In that case, would you like to come over? I feel a bit guilty about leaving you so suddenly the other day, and I also have some new designs I'd like you to look at. You have excellent taste.'

'Flatterer!' Kelly laughed.

'Well, you have.'

'I don't think I can come today.' She explained about her father.

'Then just pop over for an hour,' Maggie suggested. 'After all, your father is asleep, and Jordan is out.'

'I suppose so,' Kelly said slowly. 'Okay,' she came to a decision, 'I'll be there in fifteen minutes.'

She hurried upstairs to change out of her casual clothing into one of the stylish dresses hanging up in her wardrobe. Maggie always dressed well, at all times, and consequently Kelly always liked to dress well herself when in her company.

'I'm just going out for an hour, Mrs McLeod,' she popped into the kitchen to tell the housekeeper. 'My father shouldn't wake up before then, the doctor said the tablets should make him sleep for several hours.'

'What do I tell Mr Lord if he should come back while you're out?'

If he should come back! Mrs McLeod had also obviously been aware of Jordan's anxiety when she had arrived late back two days ago. What the housekeeper couldn't know was of Kelly's own anxiety about Jordan's delay today.

Kelly gave a casual shrug. 'Tell him I'll only be an hour.' She refused to let the housekeeper tell him where she was going. Let him worry for a while!

Maggie's flat was as dramatic as the rest of her, abstract pictures on the stark white-painted walls, the furniture very square in design, all sharp angles, scatter rugs on the black and white tiled floor. Maggie herself was a flame of colour against the black and white background, the red linen dress a series of panels ending in a ragged hem. She looked wild and gypsyish, her beautiful face glowing with pleasure as she greeted Kelly.

'You look tired.' She held Kelly at arm's length.

Colour flooded her cheeks. She looked tired because she was tired; it had been the early hours of the morning before she and Jordan had fallen asleep.

'I was hoping you would cheer me up,' she derided, 'not tell me how bad I look!'

'I didn't say bad,' Maggie bustled her into the lounge and put a drink in her hand before Kelly even knew what was happening. 'Just tired. Hey, you and Jordan haven't——'

'Maggie!' Kelly stiffened. 'If you're going to ask what I think you are, then don't. The subject is still personal.'

Maggie gave her a speculative look. 'I don't like the sound of that. Surely you haven't let him seduce you again?'

'No, I haven't!' She drank the fluid in her glass straight down, choking as the whisky burnt down into her stomach. 'God, you could have warned me!' she coughed, standing up as Maggie thumped her on the back. 'You know I don't drink whisky.' She put the glass down on the table, only half the whisky left.

'I forgot,' Maggie shrugged. 'All right now?' she asked as Kelly stopped choking.

Kelly blinked the tears away. 'I think so,' she grimaced.

'Come and look at these designs, then.' Maggie went over to her work-table, leafing through the sketches there. 'Here, and this one too. And this.' She collected quite a pile of the drawings and brought them over.

Kelly looked at them almost gratefully, picking out one or two that she might have liked for herself. At least this had taken Maggie's mind off the relationship between Jordan and herself. Not that Jordan would approve of these designs. She had bought a couple of dresses from Maggie that she could use as maternity dresses, their floating style feminine and modern but still useful as maternity dresses. Jordan had taken one look at them and thrown them out.

'They're lovely,' she told Maggie.

'Mm, I'm quite proud of them myself. I have a boutique interested in them.'

'That's great,' Kelly enthused, glad that Maggie wasn't going to ask her if she wanted any of them. She had the feeling Jordan's reaction would be the same as in the past.

'A select boutique,' Maggie added hastily. 'Each dress will be exclusively made.'

'Lovely.' Kelly listened halfheartedly as Maggie went into details, wondering if Jordan had returned home yet, and if he had if he had discovered the newspaper's source.

'Of course, if I do sign this contract with them,' Maggie continued, 'it will mean I can't go back to the States for several years.'

'But your father's offered to open your own boutique!'

'Exactly!' her friend sighed.

'I take it you didn't poison your boy-friend the other night,' Kelly remarked dryly, guessing Maggie's indecision about returning to America.

'You mean is he still around? Oh yes, even more so. He wants to move in.'

Kelly raised her eyebrows. 'Do you want him to?'

'You bet,' Maggie grinned. 'But I'm not going to appear too eager. He's too used to having things his own way. I'll give in—eventually.'

'Are you going to marry him?' Kelly asked eagerly.

'Your naïveté again, Kelly,' her friend shook her head mockingly. 'Of course I'm not going to marry him. Besides, he's already married.'

'I see,' Kelly said faintly. 'And doesn't his wife mind?'

Maggie shrugged. 'I have no idea.'

'Don't you care?' Kelly was amazed at her friend's attitude. Maggie had always been outspoken, go-ahead, but even so this latest development shocked Kelly somewhat. Maggie had had some strange boy-friends in her time, some of them quite weird, but as far as she knew none of them had ever been married.

'She should have held on to him while she could,' Maggie dismissed callously.

Kelly bit her lip. 'Maybe. But that isn't always possible.'

Contrition washed over Maggie's often hard features. 'Oh, I'm sorry, Kelly. I didn't think.'

Kelly gave a falsely bright smile. 'That's all right, it isn't important.' She stood up. I'm pleased about your designs, and if you want to stay in England then that boutique contract sounds like the best idea.'

'But you don't approve of the other bit,' Maggie grimaced.

'It's your life,' Kelly dismissed lightly. 'After the mess I've made of mine I wouldn't presume to preach to you. Maybe your way round is better.' She gave a wan smile. 'I would certainly have seen more of Jordan if I'd been his mistress instead of his wife.'

Her friend shook her head. 'You're becoming cynical.'

'Realistic,' Kelly corrected. 'We'll meet for lunch next week, shall we?'

'Lovely,' Maggie smiled. 'And I'll let you know whether I've chosen a life of sin or if I'm going home to Mummy and Daddy. But I don't think it will be the latter.'

Kelly shouldn't really be shocked about Maggie's boyfriend being married, after all, that sort of thing had been common enough five years ago, now it was accepted as the done thing. The fact that she didn't subscribe to the belief herself was beside the point.

There was an unfamiliar car parked outside the house when she got home, plus Jordan's Mercedes, although it was the other car that held her attention. Who could their visitor be?

The sound of female laughter could be heard among the male amusement as Kelly entered the house. The sound was coming from the lounge, so she made her way there.

All laughter stopped as she entered the room. Her father was sitting in one of the armchairs Jordan in the other, and their visitor on the sofa. Kelly could only see the top of a blonde female head, and her breath caught in her throat. Surely Jordan hadn't——? Not Angela Divine!

'Ah, Kelly,' Jordan stood up, coming over to the door where she still stood. 'Darling,' he smiled, but his eyes remained hard. He bent to kiss her briefly on the lips. 'Where the hell have you been this time?' he muttered.

'You've been drinking!' He drew back, his eyes narrowed.

'Yes!' Her eyes flashed her defiance before she put her hand in the crook of his arm, turning with a bright smile to face her father and their visitor. Only it wasn't Angela Divine! This was someone new, although if anything she was even more beautiful than Jordan's ex-secretary. 'Aren't you going to introduce me, darling?' she asked her husband throatily.

'You don't need introducing to Anne, Kelly,' her father said with amusement.

'I don't?' she frowned her puzzlement.

'Anne Fellows, darling,' Jordan drawled mockingly.

Anne Fellows! Kelly hadn't even recognised the nursing Sister out of uniform. She was just too beautiful. In her uniform she had been starchily attractive, dressed as she was now in the pretty pink flower-print skirt and skimpy pink top she looked too humanly lovely, completely feminine, her blonde hair long and straight and reaching almost to her narrow waist. She must be in her early or mid-thirties, and Kelly's jealousy increased as she realised the other woman was nearer Jordan's own age.

'I'm sorry I didn't recognise you, Miss Fellows.' She forced a smile to her lips, leaving Jordan's side to go and sit beside the other woman. 'And after all you've done to help my father,' she added guiltily, her smile more genuine and relaxed now.

'That's perfectly all right,' the other woman smiled warmly. 'The uniform fools a lot of people.'

'It certainly fooled me,' Kelly's father chuckled. 'I could hardly believe my eyes today.'

Anne gave a husky laugh. 'You're very kind.'

'My father-in-law is understating the case if anything,' Jordan put in.

Anne's smile widened. 'You're even kinder.'

'Jordan isn't kind,' Kelly's voice was brittle. 'He merely

knows a very beautiful woman when he sees one.' She turned to meet the anger in his eyes.

His mouth was tight, his expression glacial. 'I ought to, I'm married to one.'

'Why, thank you, darling.' She gave him a smile of exaggerated sweetness, turning to the other woman. 'Aren't the men being absolutely charming, Miss Fellows?'

'They certainly are. And please call me Anne. Now that your father is no longer in my care all formality can be dropped.'

Kelly wondered how far *all* meant as far as Jordan was concerned. Oh, she had to stop this, she was becoming paranoic about him. It didn't necessarily follow that every beautiful blonde he met was destined for his bed. And yet she remembered Anne Fellows' interest in him from the start, and he made no effort to hide his admiration for her now.

The other woman stood up, her legs smooth and shapely, slightly tanned, and completely bare. 'I have to be on my way now, I'm on duty soon,' she said regretfully.

Kelly's father stood up too. 'It's very kind of you to offer me a lift. I'll just get my jacket.'

'But——' Kelly frowned her puzzlement. 'Where are you going?'

'To the hospital,' her father replied cheerfully. 'Dr Jones has decided to do some more tests on me.'

'But this morning——'

'I rang him, Kelly,' her father said gently. 'As I started to wake up this afternoon I have a vague recollection of remembering something. The doctor wants to see how far it goes.'

Still she frowned. 'And he sent Miss Fellows—Anne, in her spare time, to collect you?'

'No,' the nurse laughed. 'I was driving over this way, so I offered.'

Once again suspicion flared within Kelly. This woman's explanation didn't ring true. Why would an important part of a medical team drive out here to pick up a patient, even if she was in the area? There had to be a motive behind her actions, and that motive was Jordan!

'That was—very kind of you,' she said jerkily.

'Oh, Anne is known for her kindness,' Jordan said deeply, rather pointedly Kelly thought.

'I'll get my jacket,' Kelly's father repeated. 'I won't be a moment.'

'I'll wait outside in the car for you,' Anne Fellows called out to him.

'Fine,' he turned to smile. 'I can get a taxi back when I'm through.'

'Are you sure you wouldn't like me to drive you?' Kelly asked him. 'I could wait with you and drive you back.'

He shook his head. 'I don't know how long I'll be. I don't want to keep you waiting around for hours.'

'Oh, I wouldn't mind——'

'Let the man go off with a beautiful woman, Kelly,' Jordan interrupted firmly. 'At his age he won't get many more opportunities,' he added mockingly.

'At his age?' Anne Fellows frowned. 'But I don't understand, he's only——'

'Private joke,' Kelly's father explained. 'I'll tell you about it on the way to the hospital.'

The nurse shrugged, turning to look at Kelly and Jordan. 'It was nice to meet you both again. Perhaps I'll see you again some time,' she smiled.

'I'd take bets on it,' Jordan smiled back, a smile that tugged at Kelly's heartstrings. It was a smile completely without mockery or cruelty, the sort of smile he had once given her.

'You'd take bets on it!' Kelly stormed once they were alone, the slamming of the front door telling of her father's departure. 'You know damn well it's a certainty.'

'As long as you do too . . .'

'Oh, I do,' she snapped. 'I'm certainly not as blind as you think I am.'

'Don't you like her?' he raised his eyebrows.

'Yes, I like her! Is that supposed to make a difference?'

'It should do.'

'Well, it doesn't. Now what else did you find today apart from Anne Fellows?' she asked caustically. 'Or was she the leak to the papers?'

'Don't be absurd,' Jordan dismissed impatiently. 'I found out damn all,' he scowled. 'No one was willing to tell me a thing, about Ben Durston or how he got his information. I spent all morning trying to get someone to talk to me, and then I had a boring lunch with an editor who had no intention of telling me a thing, except that Ben Durston is freelance, and that he occasionally comes up with an exclusive like this. Which is probably the reason for their silence—he must be invaluable.' His mouth twisted.

'So we're no further forward?'

'No.'

'Why didn't you telephone and let us know you wouldn't be back for lunch?' she asked waspishly.

'Probably for the same reason you refused to tell Mrs McLeod where you were going,' he said tautly. 'I didn't consider it any of your business.'

'I didn't refuse to tell Mrs McLeod where I was going! I told her I would be out for an hour, I didn't realise I had to report my every move. Lunch was different,' she insisted at his pointed glance. 'You caused a great deal of inconvenience.'

'Mrs McLeod told me that it was salad for lunch,'

Jordan taunted. 'Hardly an inconvenience.'

'It was to me,' Kelly said tightly.

'Where have you been this afternoon, Kelly?' he demanded grimly.

'Out.'

'Out where?'

She faced him defiantly. 'Just out.'

'You've been drinking,' he said harshly.

'Only——'

'Haven't you?' he demanded fiercely, his body taut.

He was in a dangerous mood, Kelly could tell that. And yet she didn't care, feeling in a rather tense mood herself. 'Yes, I have. What has that to do with you?'

He moved toward her. 'Who were you drinking with? Who, Kelly?'

'M-Maggie,' she faltered, his glittering eyes and bared teeth telling her of his knife-edge emotions. 'I was drinking with Maggie,' she repeated nervously.

'Liar!' he rasped. 'You've been with some man this afternoon, haven't you? Who was he, Kelly? What's the name of your lover?'

She swallowed hard. 'I don't have a lover. I told you I don't, that I never have had.'

'You lied to me,' he told her fiercely. 'Did he take you to his home or to a hotel?'

'I've been to Maggie's!' she insisted. 'Honestly I have.'

'I don't believe you,' he ground out.

'But I have. Call her. Call her, Jordan,' she suggested desperately, realising she had woken an anger inside him that she had never seen before.

His mouth twisted with bitter humour. 'Call that witch? You have to be joking! She'd tell me any old rubbish if she thought it would get to me. You've probably covered this alibi with her, anyway.'

'No, Jordan,' Kelly's tone was almost pleading, his fingers biting suddenly into her arms. 'I really was with her.'

'You've been drinking whisky—you never drink whisky.'

'It was an accident. I didn't realise——'

'You're lying to me, Kelly. Lying!' He shook her.

'No, no, I'm not. Maggie gave me the whisky and I drank it without realising. I—What are you doing?' she cried as he swung her up into his arms. 'Jordan, where are you taking me?' she demanded to know as he started to stride out of the room.

'Upstairs,' he told her grimly, a determined glitter to his eyes.

'Up——? What for?' She began to struggle.

The smile he gave wasn't pleasant. 'Why do you think?' he taunted, walking easily up the stairs, even with her weight in his arms.

Kelly swallowed hard, more frightened now than she cared to admit. 'No, Jordan,' she pleaded, now realising his intent. 'Not like this!'

'Exactly like this,' his teeth were bared in a threat. 'I know of only one way of getting the truth out of you. Before I've finished with you I'll have you begging to tell me where you really went this afternoon—and who with,' he added tautly.

Kelly had never seen Jordan like this before, had never seen that wild glitter in his eyes, this hard unyielding anger that made her quake. And she had no doubt that while he might have liked to beat her his actual physical chastisement would come in a totally diffferent way from violence. Jordon intended making love to her until she relaxed all her barriers.

CHAPTER SEVEN

JORDAN was dressing with jerky movements, his muscled back firmly turned towards Kelly as he sat on the side of the bed. Kelly resisted the impulse to reach out and touch that rippling flesh; Jordan's mood was still an unknown quantity to her.

She lay beneath the sheet, the clothes she had been wearing until an hour ago scattered all over the floor where Jordan had thrown them. Kelly thought that one or two of these garments would be damaged beyond repair—Jordan's impatience had not allowed for buttons and catches.

What had followed this frenzied removal of her clothes had been totally unlike anything she and Jordan had ever shared before. Jordan had made love to her as if he wanted her body only, with none of his usual gentle arousal in evidence. In the end he had Kelly clinging to him unashamedly, eagerly telling him everything he wanted to know about this afternoon. Finally he had seemed to accept that her visit to Maggie was the truth, but still he took her without evident emotion.

Kelly loved every second of his possession, knowing that she loved him and wanted the physical intimacy his nearness brought. But Jordon had turned away from her the moment their heartbeats steadied, and he was even now dressing to leave her.

'Jordan . . .' her voice was tentative.

'Yes?' the single word rapped out angrily.

'Do you believe me now?' She at last dared to touch the warmth of his back, instantly feeling him flinch away from her. 'Jordan?' she bit her lip as he stood up.

'Yes, I believe you.' He buttoned his shirt, tucking it back into his trousers. 'There are certain circumstances under which you never lie. This was one of them,' he said harshly.

Kelly had always believed lovemaking was a way of being emotionally close to someone as well as physically, but Jordan was even more remote to her at this moment than he had ever been. And now he was leaving the room, without a single word to say to her.

When he had gone she collapsed against the pillows in a fit of uncontrollable weeping. He had just proved, in the most humiliating way possible, that she was still just a body to him. She couldn't let it continue, not under these circumstances. She would ask Mrs McLeod to prepare a separate bedroom for Jordan tonight.

Her father returned from the hospital just before dinner, and Kelly took the opportunity to see the housekeeper while the two men were having a pre-dinner drink.

'Oh, but it's already been arranged,' the housekeeper assured Kelly at her request.

She blinked hard. 'It has?'

'Yes. Mr Lord spoke to me about it earlier.'

Kelly paled. 'He did?'

'Mm,' Mrs McLeod nodded. 'He explained that his insomnia is disturbing you.'

Jordan's lack of sleep did disturb her, but not in the way he had implied to the housekeeper! 'I see,' she bit her lip, giving a strained smile. 'Well, as long as it's been sorted out. I—I think I'll join the men in the lounge. Excuse me,' and she hurriedly made her escape.

So Jordan didn't want to share her bed any more either. Her appeal had waned much sooner this time. Thank goodness she had been spared the humiliation of telling him she still loved him. At least he wouldn't have been able to realise the truth of her emotions, not with the cool way she had been treating him when they weren't in bed together, making light of the times they were.

She couldn't face Jordan at the moment, she needed time to hide her despair from his piercing gaze. He was too shrewd at discerning her mood, and while she would have found great pleasure denying him access to her bedroom, to have him be the one to instigate such a move she found hard to bear.

She was just retouching her lipstick when Jordan came into the bedroom a few minutes later. She was very pale, the lipstick a vivid splash of colour in her face, her movements jerky and unco-ordinated.

'Your father is waiting to go in to dinner,' he told her in a stilted voice.

'I'm sorry,' she said coolly. 'I'm ready to go down now.'

'Kelly . . .' Jordan stopped her, sighing. 'You can stop looking so damned scared, I'm not about to repeat the events of this afternoon. In fact, you won't be bothered by my presence in here any longer. I shall be sleeping in one of the other rooms tonight, and every other night that I stay here.'

His words were a warning of his intention of moving out as soon as her father was completely well. She had expected as much, but he had just confirmed it. 'That suits me,' she told him carelessly.

'I thought it might,' his mouth twisted.

'Shall we go down?' she asked lightly.

'Why not?' he shrugged, opening the door for her.

Kelly spent most of the evening talking to her father. His visit to the hospital had gone very well. 'Dr Jones wants me to spend a couple of hours there each day. He thinks it might be good therapy for me.'

'Surely it would be better therapy for you to be with

people you know?' Kelly frowned her puzzlement.

'Dr Jones says no.' Her father grinned. 'I've decided to let Miles carry on without me for a few more days.'

'So he won't be coming over now.'

'Not now I know I don't have the Landers contract to worry about. The way my memory is at the moment I don't think I would be much help if I did go in to the office. I do at least remember the rapidity with which the business world changes. I'd be like an unfledged duckling among vultures!'

'I take it I'm one of the vultures,' Jordan drawled dryly.

'The biggest,' his father-in-law smiled to take the sting out of his words. 'And the best.'

Jordan gave a mocking bow. 'I'll take that as a compliment.'

'I'm sure Daddy meant it as one,' Kelly put in abruptly. 'He's always had admiration for people who see what they want, and take it.' There was a double edge to her words, and by Jordan's expression he hadn't missed it.

'Except once,' her father said cheerfully, the underlying tension missed by him. 'I didn't appreciate him taking you away from me,' he explained at their querying looks. 'And with such haste too. It was almost indecent.'

'You're wrong about that, David,' Jordan contradicted slowly, his eyes promising Kelly retribution for her dig at him just now. 'It would only have been indecent if I *hadn't* married Kelly,' he mocked.

'What the——? Oh—oh yes,' her father laughed. 'I see what you mean.'

'Well, I don't!' Kelly snapped. 'I don't like your implication, Jordan.' She wouldn't let his insult pass uncontested.

'He's only teasing, love,' her father scolded gently.

'Well, I didn't like it!' Two bright spots of angry colour heightened her cheeks.

'Kelly doesn't like to be teased,' Jordan taunted.

'No, I don't,' her eyes flashed. 'Not about something like that.'

He held up his hands in mock defeat. 'Subject closed.'

Her father yawned tiredly. 'I'm off to bed. I'll see you two tomorrow.'

Jordan stood up once they were alone, moving to pour himself a whisky. 'I hope you're happy now that you've frightened—no, frightened is the wrong word, embarrassed is more appropriate. I hope you're happy now that you've embarrassed your father into going to bed.'

'*I* didn't do that,' she gasped. 'You did. You implied that you did me a favour by marrying me.'

'Did I?' Jordan's mouth quirked in a mocking smile. 'I think you must have misunderstood me.'

'I didn't misunderstand anything,' Kelly scorned. 'You more or less told my father that if we hadn't got married you would still have got to sleep with me.'

'Did I?' he repeated infuriatingly.

'You know damn well you did!' she snapped, standing angrily to her feet. 'You conceited swine! I wouldn't have slept with you. I wouldn't have——'

'Wouldn't you?' he cut in coldly. 'I seem to remember a few occasions when you pleaded differently.'

'You bastard!' she stormed. 'You don't forget a damn thing, do you? You weren't so unmoved yourself!'

'I've never denied it,' he acknowledged abruptly. 'Whereas you do it all the time.'

'I hate you!' she glared at him fiercely. 'I hate you!'

Jordan shrugged. 'That's nothing new.'

Her bottom lip trembled at his completely emotionless tone. 'I always did bore you,' she choked.

'You never bored me,' he denied grimly.

'Got on your nerves, then. It amounts to the same thing.'

His mouth twisted. 'You said I never took the time to know you, it seems you never bothered to get to know me either. Maybe we were just too busy protecting the inner us, too frightened to let our barriers down.'

'Frightened?' Kelly scoffed. 'You've never been frightened of anything in your life!'

He shook his head. 'You really don't know me.'

'I know the you you let me know,' she cried. 'You're the one with barriers, Jordan. I've always been easy to read.'

'Maybe you have at that.' He turned away. 'Goodnight, Kelly.'

'Good—goodnight?' she choked, the conversation far from over as far as she was concerned.

'Yes.' His back was firmly turned towards her.

'Why is it you always clam up every time we get anywhere near understanding each other?' she demanded to know.

'Because it's too late for that,' he sighed. 'Much too late. I said goodnight, Kelly,' he reminded her pointedly.

She swallowed hard, frustrated with his attitude. Why wouldn't he talk to her, at least tell her he despised her if he did? He was a man made out of granite, needing a woman in his life only as a means of appeasing a natural body function, having no use for her outside of that section of his life. Kelly realised now that in the past she must have intruded, had demanded more than Jordan was prepared to give. And she had started to do it again, that was the reason he had once again rejected her. Thank God she hadn't agreed to go back to him on a permanent basis; her attraction had lasted even less time than it had before.

Sleep wouldn't come to her. She had become used to the lean strength of Jordan's body entwined with hers, had felt comforted and protected in his arms. The bed now seemed big and lonely, a poignant reminder of how things had been for them after she had told him about the baby.

She shouldn't have thought of the baby. Thinking of the baby brought Angela Divine back into her mind too, especially that last conversation she had heard between Jordan and the other girl. Kelly rolled over in the bed, her face buried in the pillow that still had a faint smell of Jordan's aftershave and the cheroots he smoked. The conversation between Jordan and his secretary was indelibly printed in her brain, each hurtful, shocking word engraved in her memory.

'If she finds out she won't like it.' Jordan's voice had been lazily amused.

Kelly had been in the process of entering the office, but something had held her back. If she had walked in she would have been confronted with guilty faces, although no doubt Jordan would have carried off the moment with his usual arrogance.

Angela had given a husky laugh, completely confident. 'She won't find out. There's absolutely no reason why she should.'

'You obviously don't know her very well, she's a very possessive young lady.' Jordan still sounded amused. 'And her father is very influential in the business world. There could be trouble.'

'That wouldn't stop us meeting,' Angela declared.

'I guess it wouldn't at that,' Jordan had laughed. 'You're very sure of yourself, Angela.'

'Shouldn't I be?' The secretary's voice was huskily suggestive.

'Yes, I think maybe you should.'

Angela gave a throaty laugh. 'I know my own potential.'

'With good reason, I should say,' Jordan said softly.

'Jordan,' Angela's voice was persuasive, 'do you think before Kelly has her baby we could take some time off to go away together? I realise it won't be possible after that, you'll be too busy.'

'I suppose I could arrange a couple of days. Okay, Angie, you make the arrangements and let me know when you want to go.'

'Oh, thank you, Jordan!' Angela had cried ecstatically. 'I'll go and do that now.'

That had been the moment Kelly had come to her senses, the moment she had run sobbing from the building, the reason she couldn't even bear Jordan near her when he came to the hospital later.

Kelly groaned, the memories as painful as if it had been yesterday. It was no good, she would never sleep now. She got up and dressed in denims and a warm jumper, and crept softly down the stairs. Maybe a walk would help relax her, taken her mind off these deep, dark thoughts.

London was strangely silent this time of the morning; a few people were still on the streets, but it was nowhere near as crowded as it always was during the day. Kelly enjoyed her window-shopping, ignoring the attempts of several men to pick her up. After all, she must look very suspect wandering around the streets, obviously aimlessly. The men took their rebuffs goodnaturedly, although Kelly was wise enough to realise she might not be as fortunate the next time, turning for home, her purposeful steps precluding anyone talking to her this time.

It was after four o'clock in the morning when she let herself back into the house and went to the kitchen to take herself a much-needed cup of coffee.

It was strangely eerie sitting in the silence of the stainless-steel kitchen. She felt like the only person awake in the world, like—what was that? She had heard a noise from somewhere in the house. Surely no one else was awake this early in the morning? Perhaps it was her father, unable to sleep because of the terrible shock he had received earlier.

There it was again, and it sounded like a groan this time. Oh lord, she thought, he wasn't ill again, was he?

She traced the noise to Jordan's study. What on earth was her father doing in there? The door creaked as she slowly pushed it open, disturbing the man sprawled across the couch, an empty bottle of whisky lying beside him on the carpeted floor beside him. Jordan!

Kelly walked over to him. The room reeked of whisky, some of it was actually spilt on the floor if she wasn't mistaken, which should please the housekeeper. Jordan groaned once again as she touched his shoulder, his eyes flickering open, their grey depths bleary and unfocusing as he blinked up at her.

'Wh—what do you want?' his voice was slurred. 'Why can't you stay away from me? Leave me alone. Go away, I tell you!' He feebly struck out at her.

'I will not!' she said angrily, shaking him as his eyes began to close. 'Wake up, Jordan. Come on,' she pulled at his arm. 'You can't stay here.'

'I can stay where I damn well please,' he scowled at her.

'You should be in bed,' she told him impatiently.

His expression was scornful. 'What's the point, you won't share it with me.'

Deep colour flooded her cheeks. 'Go to bed, Jordan,' she said tightly.

He turned over, closing his eyes. 'I'm perfectly com—com—I'm all right where I am,' he amended sleepily.

'Jordan!' Kelly shook him again. 'Jordan, wake up,' she ordered desperately, but made no impression on his drunken state.

Her father suddenly appeared in the doorway, taking in the situation at a glance. 'Need any help?' he asked gently.

Kelly gave him a grateful smile. 'Could you help me get him to bed? He—he isn't well,' she blushed.

A taunting laugh was emitted from Jordan, despite his having seemed to have been asleep. 'What Kelly means,' he rolled over, almost falling off the edge of the couch, 'is that I'm stoned out of my mind,' and he laughed again.

Her father came into the room, his dark hair tousled, a bathrobe covering his navy blue pyjamas. 'I didn't realise you were having a party,' he said dryly.

'Oh yes,' Jordan looked up at him with wide bleary eyes. 'For one,' he gave a bitter laugh. 'Isn't that so, my love?' He gave a taunting smile in Kelly's direction. 'Tell your father the reason for my solitary party,' he encouraged, half sitting up. 'Tell him——' and he sank slowly back on to the couch, completely unconscious.

'Oh God!' Kelly buried her face in her hands. 'I'm sorry, Daddy. So sorry you had to see this.'

'That's all right, love,' he put his arm about her shoulders. 'Had an argument, did you?'

'Yes.' She hid her face against his chest.

'A bad one?'

'Quite bad.' Her voice was muffled.

'Never mind. Even the best marriages have them.' He held her at arm's length. 'Cheer up, love. No marriage is a success if you don't have the occasional argument. Think how bored you would be if you agreed about everything.'

'I suppose so,' she sniffed inelegantly. Her father couldn't possibly realise how bad things were between herself and Jordan. But why on earth had Jordan got drunk like this? It certainly wasn't because of the argument they had had. Maybe he found this pretence too restricting to his own social life. Whatever the reason, he couldn't stay here. 'We have to get him upstairs,' she told her father. 'He can't be found by Mrs McLeod in this condition.'

'No, you're right. You take one arm and I'll take the other.' He pulled Jordan up into a sitting position.

'Are you sure you're up to this?' Kelly frowned her concern.

He laughed. 'Don't worry about me, I'll be all right. I think it's Jordan you should be worrying about, he's going to have a terrible hangover when he wakes up.'

'That's no more than he deserves.'

'Bitchy!' he chided softly. 'Everyone is entitled to get drunk occasionally. Although I must say I've never seen Jordan like this before, I thought he had too much self-control.'

'Oh, he has self-control.' They hoisted him to his feet, supporting him either side as they half walked, half carried him upstairs. 'It just lapses sometimes,' although not usually in this way!

'Here we are.' Her father pushed open the bedroom door and they laid Jordan down on the bed.

Too late Kelly realised they were in the bedroom Jordan had moved out of only that afternoon. Oh well, it was too late now to worry about that. Anyway, she could never explain the use of a different bedroom to her father.

'Need any help getting him undressed?' Her father looked down at Jordan as he lay sideways across the bed.

'I don't think I'll bother,' Kelly grimaced. 'Better to let him sleep. I'll just take his shoes off,' and she proceeded to do so. 'You get back to bed, Daddy. I'll be all right now.'

'Night, love,' he bent to kiss her on the temple. 'And don't be too hard on him in the morning, he doesn't make a habit of this behaviour.'

Kelly sat in the bedroom chair watching Jordan for

what was left of the night. He muttered a lot in his sleep, incoherently most of the time, obviously disturbed.

He was still asleep when she left the bedroom to join her father for breakfast. Not that she had tried to aid his slumber, banging drawers and cupboards as she took out her denims and blouse before going into the shower. None of her movements seemed to disturb Jordan in the least, his sleep was now deep and untroubled.

'Still sleeping, is he?' her father teased as Kelly sat down at the table.

'Yes,' she acknowledged tightly.

'Probably the best thing for him.'

'Probably.' She poured herself some coffee.

'Still angry with him?' He raised his eyebrows questioningly.

'Yes.' Kelly didn't attempt to prevaricate.

'Must have been some argument.'

'It was.'

'It surely doesn't have anything to do with the way he teased you?'

'Indirectly,' she revealed abruptly.

'Oh, Kelly love, you can't——'

'Please, Daddy,' she said firmly. 'I know you mean well, but—well, I——'

'Don't interfere, hmm?' he quirked an eyebrow. 'It's all right, you can tell me if I'm out of line.'

She looked down at her cup. 'You're out of line.'

'Enough said,' he accepted goodnaturedly. 'Now, do you feel like driving me to the hospital? I've been advised not to drive for the moment.'

Kelly smiled, relieved that he didn't pursue the subject of her argument with Jordan. 'Of course I'll drive you,' she said eagerly. She had wanted to be out of the house when Jordan woke up. 'I'll pick you up later too, if you like,' she offered.

'That won't be necessary. Anne said she would drive me back.'

So the beautiful Sister Fellows wanted to see Jordan yet again! Kelly felt a sickening lurch in her stomach. Maybe the other woman was the reason Jordan had got drunk last night. He would probably have rather been with her than putting up a front for Kelly's father.

Jordan had already left for the office when Kelly returned from driving her father to his therapy class, and by Mrs McLeod's ruffled manner he had been in the foul mood Kelly had expected.

'Will my husband be back for lunch?' she asked the housekeeper.

'I—er—I don't think so,' Mrs McLeod stumbled a reply.

In other words the poor woman had been too frightened of his temper to ask him. He really was a tyrant! 'Then we'll all be out,' Kelly told her. 'My father intends eating at the hospital, so I think I'll eat out myself.'

'Very well, Mrs Lord.'

Kelly went into the lounge, obtaining the number she needed before dialling. 'Mrs Smythe, please,' she told the maid who answered the telephone. 'Mrs Lord calling.' She tapped her fingers impatiently on the coffee-table as she waited for Laura to come to the telephone.

'Kelly!' Laura cried her pleasure. 'How lovely to hear from you. And so providentially too. I'm feeling a bit down this morning,' she explained.

Kelly had been unsure of the other girl's reaction to her call and her unreserved pleasure was reassuring. 'Nothing serious, I hope?'

'No,' Laura laughed. 'Just impatience for the birth. I feel a bit like a tank at the moment! And I'm so tired. You've telephoned to arrange a meeting, I hope?'

'I thought lunch?'

'Lovely. You're a life-saver, Kelly. Just tell me when and where, and I'll be there.'

Kelly laughed at the other girl's mock desperation. The arrangements made, she rang off, the telephone instantly ringing, making her jump with surprise. 'Yes?' She snatched up the receiver.

'Kelly?' Jordan's voice came tersely down the line.

She instantly stiffened. 'Yes.'

'I called to say I wouldn't be in to lunch,' he told her abruptly.

'I already guessed that,' she said coolly. 'In fact, I've made arrangements to be out myself.'

'You have?' His voice was harsh.

Kelly bristled with resentment. 'Yes, I have. Do you have any objection?' her sarcasm was unmistakable.

'That depends on who you're lunching with,' he rasped. 'Maggie again?'

'No,' she replied uncommunicatively.

'Who, then?' he demanded to know.

'How is your head this morning?' She deliberately didn't answer his question. The arrogance of him!

'Bloody awful,' he growled. 'But then you expected that, didn't you?'

'Did I?' she asked infuriatingly. 'Yes, I suppose I did,' she mused.

'Did I say—anything after I passed out?'

Kelly frowned. 'A lot of rubbish that didn't make any sense.'

'None of it?' he asked tautly.

'Not that I can remember. Why?'

'Just curious. Most of the people I've seen get drunk seem to get very sentimental with it.'

'Not you, Jordan,' she gave a scornful laugh. 'Don't worry, you didn't give away any of your secrets.'

'Secrets?' Jordan echoed sharply.

'Which woman you're seeing at the moment,' she said carelessly, amazed at her talent for acting. If he had so much as mentioned another woman's name she would have scratched his eyes out. As it was, it had all been a lot of disjointed mumblings, none of which made the slightest bit of sense.

'I'm more interested in the man you're seeing,' he told her grimly. 'Who is he?'

'That's none of your business. But I'll tell him of your interest. It should amuse him,' she added before slowly replacing the receiver.

She was in her bedroom by the time the telephone began ringing again, hastily shutting herself in the bathroom as Mrs McLeod knocked on the bedroom door.

When she received no answer she had obviously come into the bedroom, and now she was knocking on the bathroom door. 'Mr Lord on the telephone, madam.'

Kelly smiled her glee. 'Could you tell him I'm in the bath, Mrs McLeod,' she called through the dividing door. 'If it's important perhaps you could take a message.' She bit her lip to stop herself laughing, imagining Jordan's fury.

The housekeeper returned a few minutes later, by which time Kelly really had run herself a bath. 'No message, Mrs Lord,' she called out to her.

She didn't think there would be. Jordan wasn't the type of man to conduct a conversation through a third person. Although she had no doubt he would demand some honest answers from her this evening. The wait would do him good.

Laura was even more glowing than before, although obviously becoming more and more ungainly as each day passed. 'I really am grateful that you called,' she smiled as she gingerly sat down. 'Ian's been so busy lately, and I've been so tense. I can't seem to settle to anything. I've been knitting a pair of bootees the last three weeks, I don't think I'll ever finish them.'

Kelly laughed. 'You will. Anyway, I'm sure you have plenty already.'

'Not really—just a couple of dozen pairs!' Laura grimaced. 'All Ian's twenty aunts seem to have made us a pair,' she confided.

'*Twenty* aunts?'

'Well—four, actually. It just seems like twenty at times. They brought him up, you see, between the four of them. When Ian's parents died they all took over his care. Oh, they're darlings really, just very possessive. Still, at least we'll have four volunteers for baby-sitting.' Laura sighed. 'If I talk too much, Kelly, just tell me. Ian says I talk much too much.'

'I like to hear it,' Kelly smiled, finding her liking for this girl increasing by the minute.

'Oh, good,' Laura grinned. 'Because I do it all the time. I'm a compulsive talker, mainly about Ian, although lately it's been about the baby. Men get so bored with baby talk, though.'

'Yes,' Kelly acknowledged with a certain amount of bitterness.

'Ian told me about your baby,' Laura said gently, compassion in her eyes. 'It was such a pity.'

'It was a long time ago.' Kelly forced a smile to her lips.

'And at least you and Jordan are back together again now.'

'That was all thanks to your husband.'

'Ian?' Laura frowned. 'What did he do?'

'He told Jordan that I needed him.' Kelly went on to explain about the accident.

'And that brought you and Jordan back together.' Laura's eyes glowed with excitement. 'How romantic!'

'Yes,' Kelly agreed dully.

'I think all marriages have their ups and downs.'

'I suppose so, although Jordan and I——' she broke off, her stricken gaze fixed on the man and woman who had just entered the restaurant and were even now being conducted to their table.

Laura instantly noticed her paleness. 'What is it?' She sat forward. 'Kelly, what's wrong?'

'I—It—I can't——' Kelly broke off again, feeling sick with reaction.

Laura followed her gaze, watching too as Jordan pulled out a chair for Anne Fellows to sit down.

CHAPTER EIGHT

So she had been right, Anne Fellows was the latest woman in Jordan's life! And it looked as if Kelly's father had been out of luck with his lift. Jordan had obviously invited the nurse out to lunch instead.

Laura was giving Kelly a searching look. 'Kelly?' she frowned her puzzlement.

'I—er—Would you mind if we went somewhere else?' She picked up her handbag in preparation of leaving.

'Of course not, if you would rather,' Laura instantly agreed.

'I would,' Kelly said tautly, rising to her feet.

She deliberately left the restaurant through a different door from the one Jordan had entered by, watching him to make sure he didn't see her. He didn't, totally engrossed in the conversation of his companion. Kelly had never felt so defeated, so totally lost to Jordan. This time it was even worse than before. Her rather immature eighteen-year-old love had developed into the all-consuming love of a woman—and Jordan was doing his best to destroy that too.

'Kelly . . .?'

She turned to face Laura. 'Sorry,' she gave a bright smile. 'I—er—I didn't want to talk to Jordan right now. He—he looked busy,' she excused, her face fiery red.

Laura pulled her towards a waiting taxi. 'Come on,' she pushed her inside. 'We'll eat at my place. That is, if you feel like eating.'

'I don't.' Kelly bit her lip to stop it trembling, the memory of Jordan's hand resting at the back of Anne

Fellows' waist still with her.

'I didn't think so. We'll talk when we get to the house,' Laura added gently.

Laura's lounge overlooked the garden, the view very soothing, almost not seeming like London. Kelly sat down before she fell down, her hands kneeding together in her lap.

'Coffee, Sue,' Laura told the maid. 'Are you sure you don't want anything to eat, Kelly?'

'No, thank you,' Kelly replied dully.

'Just coffee,' Laura requested of the maid. 'Now,' she went to sit next to Kelly on the sofa once they were alone, 'do you want to tell me about it?'

Kelly pulled herself together, on the outside at least. 'There's nothing to tell,' she said firmly.

'When you don't want to see or speak to your own husband then there's something wrong,' Laura contradicted.

Kelly's eyes flashed deeply violet. 'It wasn't a question of that, I just didn't want—didn't want him to *know* I'd seen him.'

'Why?'

She gave a casual shrug. 'I told you, he looked busy.'

'Doing what?' Laura scorned. 'Who was the woman, Kelly?'

'A nurse. She—she looked after my father.' Kelly couldn't see any point in prevaricating any longer, Laura was well aware of her distress. 'I think she's transferred her attention to Jordan now.' She gave a shaky smile.

'But you aren't sure?'

'What other explanation could there be?' she said bitterly.

'Any number of them, I would have thought.'

Kelly's mouth twisted. 'You don't know Jordan.

Besides, he has no reason to meet her, other than the obvious one.'

'Don't you think you should ask him?' Laura suggested softly.

She shook her head. 'There's no need. I already knew about them, seeing them together only confirmed it.'

'I see.' Laura smiled at the maid as she entered with the tray.

'You should have something to eat,' Kelly told her new friend. 'You have to keep your strength up.'

'I suppose so. Just a sandwich,' Laura told the young girl. 'The usual,' she added ruefully.

'The usual?' Kelly queried teasingly as the maid left.

Laura gave a selfconscious smile. 'Ham and strawberry jam.'

'Ugh!' Kelly winced.

'I know,' she grinned. 'Ian cringes every time I ask for one.'

'I'm not surprised!'

'We were talking about you,' Laura reminded her pointedly.

'No, we weren't, we were talking about Jordan. They're two totally different subjects?'

'They are?'

'Totally,' Kelly nodded.

'Then you aren't really back together?' Laura asked shrewdly.

'No.'

'I thought not,' Laura sighed. 'Don't get me wrong, it's just that when we last met you didn't exactly act like someone who was ecstatically happy. And having just been reunited with your husband I would have thought you would have been.'

Kelly smiled. 'You aren't just a pretty face, are you, there's a brain there as well.'

'I hope so,' Laura laughed. 'My father's teaching, I'm afraid. He was one of those people who believe that if you want something you should go out and get it.'

Kelly sobered. 'If you mean I should set out to capture Jordan, then it's too late. Maybe it was always too late for us.'

'Now that I don't believe. Ian told me Jordan was always besotted with you.'

Kelly gave a disbelieving laugh. 'Ian must have the wrong man. Jordan doesn't care for anyone very long, he never has done.'

'But Ian said——'

'Then he was wrong,' Kelly cut in harshly. 'I know my husband. I'm not even his type,' she added bitterly.

'Don't be silly,' Laura scorned. 'Men don't have a *type*.'

'Jordan does. Tall, leggy, and blonde.'

'Then I can understand why he married you. Yes, I can,' Laura insisted. 'You must have knocked him for six.'

'I knocked him for six months,' Kelly corrected. 'That was exactly the amount of time our marriage lasted.'

'Your fault or his?'

'A bit of both, I suppose. Heavens, you aren't really going to eat that, are you?' she said disgustedly as Laura's sandwich arrived.

'Of course,' her friend grinned. 'Look the other way if you can't bear it.'

Kelly did so. 'At least my craving was for something sensible. Chocolate biscuits,' she explained.

Laura made a face. 'How boring!'

'But not as revolting as that!'

'Don't knock it until you've tried it.' Laura bit into the sandwich with obvious enjoyment.

Just the thought of it made Kelly shudder. 'No, thanks!'

'You're evading the issue again. Help yourself to coffee,'

Laura invited. 'Now tell me what part was Jordan's fault and what part was yours.'

Kelly sighed. 'There isn't much to tell. While I was carrying Jordan's child he was having an affair with another woman.' Her hand shook as she raised the coffee cup to her lips.

'Nasty!'

'When I found out I lost the baby. After that I couldn't even bear him near me. I decided there was no point in continuing the marriage when I couldn't even stand him touching me, so I walked out.'

'You left him because you didn't like him touching you?' Laura frowned.

'Yes.'

'But didn't you realise your reaction was due to the loss of the baby and not to an actual aversion to Jordan?'

Kelly gave a wan smile. 'I do now.'

'You do?—Oh,' Laura said meaningly. 'You still love him, hmm?'

'Insanely. I have to be insane to put up with the way he treats me. I think Anne Fellows really means something to him, though, he got drunk over her last night.'

'Is that all? That's nothing unusual.'

Kelly's eyes widened. 'It isn't?'

'No.'

'What do you mean?'

'Just that he and Ian used to go out on terrific binges together when Ian and I were first dating.'

'*Jordan* did?' Kelly was incredulous.

'Mm. The first half a dozen times I met him he was absolutely plastered.'

'I find that hard to believe,' Kelly dismissed.

'But he was,' Laura insisted. 'I didn't like him very much at first. Then I met him when he wasn't drunk. He can be quite charming then.'

'I just can't believe he was drunk. I'd never seen him that way before last night.'

Laura shrugged. 'It's the truth, ask Ian. Or ask Jordan.'

Her expression hardened. 'I doubt we'll be talking for much longer.'

'Are you going to leave him again?'

'Eventually. I won't share, Laura, it isn't in my nature.'

'Or mine,' Laura admitted ruefully. 'Ian and I had a break-up before we even got married. I found out he had been two-timing me. I soon sorted that nonsense out.'

Kelly couldn't help smiling. 'You really are deceptive to look at. Underneath all that sweetness there's a steely heart.'

'You can believe it,' Laura smiled back.

'Oh, I do,' Kelly frowned. 'Are you sure Jordan wasn't just fatigued when you met him? Complete tiredness and drunkenness can often be confused.'

'He was roaring drunk.'

Kelly just couldn't believe it. It just didn't sound like that Jordan she knew, the man always in control, never allowing his emotions to rule his head. She shrugged. 'If you say so.'

'I do,' Laura grinned.

'I'll have to go now, Kelly said, getting up. 'My father should be back from the hospital, and I don't like leaving him alone too long.'

'But you'll call me again?' the other girl said eagerly. 'And we're still waiting to hear from Jordan about your coming to dinner. He did agree, didn't he?'

'Oh yes. Although I'm not sure of his plans now that he's interested in Anne Fellows. He can be pretty single-minded about such things,' Kelly said with remembered bitterness.

'Oh, but you must come, and soon. I don't have much longer to go.'

'I'll see what I can do,' Kelly promised. 'And I'll call you later in the week about another luncheon date. Although if you're going to order ham and jam sandwiches I don't think I want to go!'

Laura laughed. 'I'll be on my best behaviour, I promise.'

Kelly's thoughts were all confused on the drive back home. Jordan never drank in excess, except for last night she had never seen him in the least incapacitated, and yet Laura seemed to think it was a common occurrence. And then there had been the shock of seeing him with Anne Fellows, their intimacy evident as they bent their heads close together while talking. No wonder Jordan hadn't noticed *her*, he had been completely engrossed in the beauty of the other woman.

She was surprised to see his car in the driveway when she arrived home, having expected him to spend the afternoon with Anne Fellows too. Perhaps the other woman was on duty. What a pity, she thought bitchily.

Jordan came out of his study as she entered the house, his dark business suit removed and replaced by faded denims and an open-necked checked shirt. He looked very virile and attractive, although a trifle pale under his tan, deep lines grooved into the side of his nose and mouth.

Kelly looked away with an indifferent flicker of her eyes. 'Where's my father?' she asked coolly, walking through to the lounge.

Jordan followed her, his steely gaze boring into her. 'What sort of greeting is that?'

She eyed him defiantly. 'The only sort you're going to get from me.'

He made an impatient gesture. 'I'm sorry about my behaviour last night,' he ground out.

'If only it were just last night's behaviour!'

'What do you mean?' His expression was watchful.

She shrugged. 'It isn't important.'

He swung her round to face him. 'I'm sick of being fobbed off with those sort of remarks. I asked you a question, I want an answer.'

'I gave you one.'

'You gave me nothing!' His fingers bit into her arm. 'You never have. Everything I've ever wanted from you I've had to take. And I'm going to take now if you don't answer me,' he told her grimly.

'You wouldn't dare!' She glared at him.

'Are you challenging me, Kelly?' he asked softly, suddenly still.

'Yes!'

'Right!' He marched her out of the room and up the stairs by his hand on her nape. 'Strip,' he ordered once they were in the bedroom.

'I will not!' she told him indignantly.

Jordan's hand came out to grasp the neckline of her dress, pulling downwards with a sharp tug, and the buttons flew everywhere as the dress gaped open all the way down the front. 'Will you take off the rest or shall I?'

'Neither.' She grabbed her housecoat. 'You can't treat me like this!'

'I can't?' He took a threatening step towards her.

'No,' she trembled. 'My father——'

'Is sedated in his room,' he finished mockingly. 'Apparently he had a disturbed night.'

'And we both know why, don't we!' she said disgustedly.

He shrugged. 'You should have left me where I was, no one asked you to interfere.'

'I suppose you would rather have the staff find you that way,' she scorned.

'It wouldn't be the first time,' he drawled.

Kelly frowned. It seemed Jordan was confirming what Laura had already told her. 'Do you make a habit of being drunk?'

'Not a habit, no. Now are you going to take off the rest of your clothes or not?'

'Not,' she told him firmly.

'Then I'll take them off for you,' and he began to do so, easily holding off her flaying fists. 'You deliberately got into the bath this morning,' he continued to talk as he undressed her with studied determination, 'just so that you didn't have to speak to me.' He had her naked now.

'Why should you care?' she spat the words at him.

Jordan's mouth tightened. 'I want to know the name of the man, Kelly, the lover you keep telling me doesn't exist.' He held both her hands in one of his as he finished unbuttoning his own shirt. 'His name, Kelly!' His hold tightened on her.

'Go to hell!' she said vehemently. 'I've always believed in equality in marriage. What's good enough for you is good enough for me.'

'What are you talking about now?' he demanded impatiently.

'Don't pretend with me any longer, Jordan. I'm neither naïve nor blind.'

'You're bloody incomprehensible, that what you are,' he said angrily. 'You don't make sense half the time.'

'Well, make sense of this!' Her eyes blazed as she kicked him hard in the shin.

'You little wildcat!' He let go of her with a groan. 'You vixen!' he exclaimed furiously, beginning to come towards her.

Kelly ran. She locked the bathroom door behind her, leaning heavily back against it, jumping nervously as he rattled the door-handle. 'Go away,' she told him. 'Go away and don't ever come near me again!'

'Kelly,' his voice was huskily persuasive. 'Kelly, open
the door.'

'So you can finish what you started?' she gave a scornful
laugh. 'No way!'

'I won't touch you, I swear it.'

'You said that yesterday,' she reminded him.

She heard him sigh. 'Come out and we'll talk, nothing
else. I think it's time we talked, Kelly.'

'And I think we've run out of time. Talking between us
always ends the same way, and physical infatuation just
isn't enough for any marriage.'

'Is that all it is, physical infatuation?'

'You know it is,' she said bitterly.

There was silence for several long seconds, then Jordan
spoke again. 'If that's what you really think then you're
right, there's no point in us even talking.'

'I'm glad you realise that at last.'

'Finally and completely. I'm going now, Kelly. Come
out of there before you freeze to death.'

'Not until I'm sure you've gone!'

'You can be sure,' he said heavily. 'I won't bother you
again.' The door closed as he left.

Kelly waited several more minutes before daring to
emerge from the bathroom. The room was empty, only
her ripped clothes scattered on the floor to show Jordan's
savagery had taken place. Tears streamed down her face.
It was all over between them, finally and completely, as
Jordan had said.

Jordan kept his word and didn't come near her again.
Kelly met Laura for lunch twice during the next couple
of weeks, although the dinner had to be cancelled for some
time, as Jordan suddenly had to to away on business for a
few weeks.

While he was away Kelly felt able to relax slightly, meeting Maggie a couple of afternoons too. Her friend had signed the contract with the boutique and Maggie's boy-friend had duly moved in with her.

'When do I get to meet him?' Kelly teased one afternoon, the male articles lying about the flat evidence of his habitation.

'Meet him?' Maggie echoed sharply.

'Yes. Or aren't any of your friends going to have that privilege?'

Maggie grinned. 'I'd lock him up and throw away the key if I could.'

'You *are* in love.'

'Very much so. I'd do anything for him. As far as my parents are concerned I've already done just that—letting him move in with me. They're so old-fashioned,' she dismissed.

Then Kelly felt she must be too. Much as she loved Jordan she didn't think she could have faced the insecurity of just living with him.

When Jordan returned from his business trip he was even more cold and reserved than usual. And in the five weeks they had all been living together her father hadn't remembered a thing. He still spent a lot of time at the hospital, and had even been into the office once or twice, and yet nothing seemed to have jogged his memory.

Jordan's coldness was even harder to bear when he returned, and Kelly had no doubt he was still seeing Anne Fellows; his absence the evening of his return was evidence of that.

Kelly was in the garden when he returned from work the next evening; her father was spending the afternoon at his office.

'Do you have any plans for this evening?' Jordan came out to ask her, his business suit impeccably tailored, his shirt snowy white, his tie meticulously knotted. The strain of the last few weeks of living a dual life were beginning to show on him, the hair at his temples even greyer than before, his face much thinner too.

She had little sympathy for him, knowing she didn't look the picture of health herself. She hated sleeping alone, spent the majority of every night fighting down the urge to go to Jordan's room and beg to be taken in his arms, while he, she felt sure, spent most of his time thinking of Anne Fellows.

'Why?' she looked up to ask him.

'Because Ian Smythe has been calling me all day urging us to go to them for dinner tonight. Laura doesn't have long to go now, and she's determined to have this dinner party before she goes into hospital.'

Kelly frowned. 'I don't think that's a good idea.'

'Neither do I,' Jordan sighed. 'It's one thing putting on a show for your father, another putting one on for other people.'

'That wasn't the reason I didn't think it would be a good idea,' she said scathingly. 'I was thinking of Laura.'

'She's one determined lady. Ian's never been able to master her.'

Kelly stiffened. 'Maybe he doesn't need to. They love each other, that's enough for most people. Not all men need to assert themselves over women.'

'Meaning I do,' he said grimly.

'Always,' she agreed unhesitatingly.

'It didn't work very well with you, did it?' he snapped.

'Not at all, I would have said.'

'You could be right.'

'And you don't have to put on a show in front of anyone,' Kelly told him confidently. 'Laura is well aware of the fact that this marriage is a sham. I presume she'll have told Ian as much, they don't appear to have secrets from each other.'

'You told Laura the truth?' Jordan ignored her jibe.

'I didn't need to, she guessed.'

'How the hell many more of your cronies know about this arrangement?' He sounded angry now.

'Laura is not a *crony*,' Kelly said indignantly. 'She's a friend. I like her very much.'

'Well, she's a definite improvement on Maggie,' he dismissed scathingly.

'As far as you're concerned that isn't a compliment, you would think Judas an improvement on Maggie!' Her eyes flashed her resentment.

His mouth twisted. 'How strange you should use that comparison.'

Her gaze sharpened. 'What do you mean?'

Jordan shrugged. 'It doesn't matter.'

'Now who's evading answering the question?' she taunted bravely.

Mockery was clearly visible in his expression. 'You can give me the same treatment if you like.'

It was the first time he had referred to the afternoon he had nearly raped her, and Kelly's face blushed fiery red. 'I don't think so,' she swung her legs off the lounger. 'What time are Ian and Laura expecting us?'

'Seven-thirty.'

'Then I'd better shower and dress.'

She made herself walk calmly across the garden and into the house, all the time knowing that Jordan was watching her every move. Oh, how she wished herself immune to him, didn't care that he no longer wanted her.

She dressed with meticulous care, wanting to look her best. Anne Fellows was beautiful, but she wasn't exactly plain herself, and she wasn't going to look like a drudge even if she had lost Jordan to the other woman. Jordan would be made to see what he was missing.

Her dress was a deep petrol blue, fitting smoothly over her hips down to just below knee length, tied at the waist with a narrow belt and fitting tautly over her uptilted breasts. Her hair glowed darkly, her make-up was light and attractive. She looked cool and sophisticated, and Jordan's eyes deepened to black as he turned to look at her, although his expression was rigidly controlled as he picked up her velvet jacket and placed it around her shoulders.

'Thank you,' she accepted coolly, moving away from him. 'I haven't seen my father this evening.'

'He's out to dinner. He called while you were changing.'

'He didn't say earlier,' she frowned, shutting off from her mind how disturbingly attractive Jordan looked in an off-white suit and black silk shirt.

'Last-minute plans, I think.' He held the car door open for her, tucking the side of her dress in as he closed it again.

The sensuous smell of his aftershave reached out and touched her in the confines of the car, too strong for her to block that out too. It stirred the senses, as did the cheroot he was smoking.

Kelly usually liked the smell of these cheroots, only tonight was different. Tonight the aroma made her feel slightly sick. 'Would you mind putting that out?' she said sharply.

He looked surprised, but instantly stubbed out the cheroot in the ashtray. 'I'm sorry, I didn't think you would mind.'

'I don't,' she shook her head. 'Not normally. It's just——'

'Just that tonight you feel differently about it,' he derided.

'Yes—I mean no. Oh, I don't know,' she licked her

suddenly dry lips. 'It's so hot in here.' Beads of perspiration were breaking out on her forhead.

Jordan gave a worried glance in her direction. 'Would you like me to open a window?'

'No. No, it doesn't matter.' She took a deep breath. 'I'll be all right in a minute.'

He slowed the car down almost to a stop. 'Would you like me to turn back?'

'No!' her voice was shrill. 'No, we'll go on,' she said more calmly. If she said yes, turn back, he would probably disappear for the evening with Anne Fellows. 'Ian and Laura are expecting us.'

'I suppose it is a little late to let them down, but if you aren't feeling well . . .'

'I'm all right now,' she insisted.

The journey to the Smythes' house seemed never-ending, and Kelly hastily got out of the car once they arrived, breathing in deep gulps of air to try and clear her head.

Jordan came round to her side of the car to take her arm, looking down at her pale face. 'I should have turned back,' he said savagely.

She forced a smile, standing erect, her head thrown back. 'I'm fine. Really.'

'You don't damn well look it,' he muttered as he ran the doorbell.

'Thanks!' Kelly said tautly. 'That's just what I wanted to hear.'

His mouth tightened. 'You know what I meant!'

'You meant I look awful.' She was feeling too ill to do more than snap at him.

'No——'

The door was opened to them by Laura herself. 'Kelly!' she hugged her. 'And Jordan,' she said more shyly.

He raised his eyebrows. 'Am I allowed to kiss my hostess?'

Laura blushed. 'Perhaps you should ask your wife that.'

He slanted Kelly a mocking glance. 'Well?'

'Kiss who you like', she shrugged. 'You always do anyway.'

He drew in a ragged breath, but said nothing as he bent to kiss Laura on the cheek. 'Not much longer to go?' he teased her rotund shape.

'Two days—officially. Unofficially, any time,' she smiled.

'Not tonight, I hope?' he said in mock horror.

She giggled. 'You never know. You go through to the lounge, Jordan. You know the way, and I'm sure Ian would love to press a glass of whisky on you.'

He smiled. 'He won't have to press very hard.'

'Kelly and I will just take her wrap upstairs.'

'Very tactful,' Kelly laughed once they reached Laura's bedroom. 'Does it really need two of us to carry a velvet jacket upstairs?'

'You know it doesn't,' her friend dismissed impatiently. 'Are things no better between you and Jordan?'

'Worse,' Kelly replied unhesitatingly.

'I'm sorry, I had hoped—Is he still seeing this other woman?'

'Yes.'

'Ian didn't believe it when I told him——'

'You told *Ian* about that?' Kelly interrupted in dismay.

'I tell him everything. And he said——'

'I don't want to know, Laura.' She put her hand through the crook of the other girl's arm. 'Let's go and eat, before I faint with hunger!'

Half way through the dessert she thought that was exactly what she was going to do. It suddenly washed over her in waves, so much so that she thought she was actually going to faint at the table.

'Do you feel sick again?' Jordan was sitting opposite her, watching her intently.

She nodded wordlessly, taking a drink of the water she had requested with her meal.

Jordan stood up to come and pull her chair back for her, helping her over to the sofa.

'I'm sorry,' she mumbled to Laura and Ian. 'I think it must have been the shellfish I ate for lunch.'

'Why the hell didn't you say so?' Jordan rasped. 'I'll call a doctor.'

'No!'

'But if you've been poisoned by this fish you could be really ill,' he reasoned firmly.

Laura came over to feel her forehead. 'She doesn't feel as if she has a fever or anything like that.'

'Nevertheless,' Jordan insisted, 'I'd rather she had a doctor, just to make sure it's nothing serious.'

'I agree with Jordan,' Ian chimed in. 'You don't mess around with things like shellfish.'

'I think all she needs is to lie down for a while,' Laura told them.

'But you aren't a doctor, darling,' her husband said gently.

'Maybe not, but I think she's right.' Kelly was embarrassed at being the centre of attention like this.

'Maybe I should just get you home and then call a doctor,' Jordan said thoughtfully.

'No!' The thought of that drive home at the moment made her feel even more sick. 'Laura's right, a lie down and I'll be fine.'

'I'm not so sure——' Still he hesitated.

Kelly looked appealingly at Laura. She just couldn't face that drive at the moment. She just wanted to be alone.

'A lie down,' Laura said firmly, answering her silent plea. 'Come on upstairs with me.'

Kelly swayed as she stood up, leaning heavily on Jordan as he put an arm about her waist to assist her. 'I'll be all right in a minute,' she assured him. 'Really I will.'

'You'd better be,' he said grimly.

The bedroom was cool and dark, and she lay down gratefully on the bed. 'I feel so silly,' she gave a wan smile, 'making a fuss like this.'

'You aren't making a fuss,' Laura told her. 'Off you go, Jordan. I'll make sure she's comfortable before I come down.'

'Kelly?' he looked down at her.

'I'm feeling better already,' she smiled up at him, heaving a sigh of relief when he reluctantly left.

Laura sat down beside her on the bed. 'How do you really feel?'

'Lousy!' she grimaced, very pale.

'I thought so. Still,' Laura stood up, 'nothing a strong cup of tea and a dry biscuit won't cure.'

Kelly gave her a sharp look, sighing heavily. 'You know, don't you?'

Laura gave her a look of feigned innocence. 'Know what?'

She sighed again. 'That I'm pregnant.'

'Yes, I know,' her friend confirmed. 'But Jordan doesn't, does he?'

'No.' Kelly bit her lip. 'I didn't know myself until tonight, until this sickness suddenly came over me. Oh, Laura, what am I going to do?' she cried desperately.

CHAPTER NINE

LAURA looked calmly down at her. 'What do you want to do?'

'I don't know,' said Kelly in confused anguish. 'It's all such a shock.'

'Don't you want the baby, is that it?'

'Not want——!' Kelly gasped. 'Of course I want the baby,' she said indignantly.

Laura shrugged. 'Then where's the problem?'

'The baby's father!'

'Jordan?'

'Well, of course Jordan!'

'Just checking,' Laura grinned.

'Well, you can stop right now. Jordan is definitely the father of my child.' Kelly sighed. 'He's been the only man ever in my life.'

'You sound regretful,' Laura probed.

'I think regretful is the wrong word. Maybe if I had been able to love someone else I wouldn't have fallen for Jordan so easily a second time, and consequently got myself into this mess.'

'Is that what you feel it is, a mess?'

'No,' she sighed again. 'Do you know what I really feel? Ecstatic!' Her eyes glowed. 'I love the thought of carrying Jordan's child again. But I won't hold on to him that way!'

'Have you ever thought of the fact that he might like to be held—any way?' Laura raised her eyebrows questioningly.

Kelly shook her head. 'He's already told me that as

soon as my father is well again he wants me out of his life,' she recalled dully.

'He actually said that?'

'Oh yes.'

'Oh,' Laura frowned, shrugging. 'I'll go and get that tea and biscuit.'

'Laura!' Kelly stopped her. 'You won't tell Jordan the real reason I was ill?'

'Of course not,' Laura scorned. 'Although you do realise it isn't something you can hide for long?'

'Mm,' Kelly grimaced. 'I was enormous at three months last time.'

Her friend nodded. 'Some women are like that. How many weeks are you?'

She flushed. 'Five.'

'You sound very sure.'

Kelly looked down at her hands. 'I am.'

'I won't be long,' and Laura left her.

She was pregnant! She wanted to shout, to scream, to cry—and all with happiness. This time nothing would go wrong, this time she would have the baby, with or without Jordan. And she meant it about not keeping him in that way. If he had shown any sign of coming to love her she might have felt differently. But if she couldn't have Jordan at least she would have his child.

She didn't need a doctor to confirm her pregnancy, and yet remembering the kindness of Paul Anderson, the specialist who had looked after her the last time, she thought she ought to go and see him. He had been excellent at his job, had always made her feel important, a person, not just a baby-producing machine as so many of these doctors did. Yes, she would make an appointment to see him.

'Here we are,' Laura arrived with the promised tea and biscuits. 'Now I'd better go down and assure that anxious husband of yours.'

Kelly sat up to drink the tea, munching slowly on the dry biscuit. How easily she had become pregnant again, how wonderfully easily. If only she could share her happiness with Jordan, could share with him the magical wonder of their child forming inside her.

But he had never found the thought of fatherhood wonderful, he had avoided even talking about their life together after the baby was born. Well, this time he would deny her none of her joy, she would cherish it to her like a cloak, a protection against the pain of losing Jordan.

Laura came quietly back into the bedroom, going to the wardrobe to pull out a tiny suitcase she had in there. She began checking the contents.

Kelly sat up, swinging her legs to the floor, the feelings of sickness and dizziness now gone. 'What are you doing?' she asked curiously.

'Just making sure I have everything,' Laura said vaguely. 'And it's a good job I did, I only seem to have put in one nightgown.' She put another two on top of the other contents of the case. 'Maybe I should put in a spare toothbrush too.'

Kelly grinned. 'I don't think the baby will need one straight away.'

She received an impatient look. 'I meant for me. I have a habit of losing them.'

'Then by all means put in a spare one,' Kelly encouraged, watching as Laura wandered into the bathroom to get one. 'Couldn't you do this some other time, Laura?' she frowned. 'You've had enough to do this evening with preparing us dinner. You should be putting your feet up.'

'I will, when I get the chance. Right, that's my case sorted out. Now I wonder if I have time to tidy the dining-room before I go?' She bit her lip thoughtfully. 'I gave Carol the evening off because I wanted to cook the meal myself, and I don't want to leave everywhere in a mess for her tomorrow. Do you think I have time to tidy up?'

'Time?' Kelly repeated dazedly. 'We can do that together, surely? I feel perfectly well now.'

Laura's expression brightened. 'Oh, good. If we go down and do it now it shouldn't take as long with the two of us.' She suddenly stopped what she was doing to take deep gasping breaths, her hand pressed to her swollen stomach. 'Oh dear,' she sighed, straightening. 'That one was quite bad.'

'*That* one?' Kelly demanded. 'What do you mean, that one?'

'I've been having contractions for the last couple of hours,' Laura told her happily.

'You have?' Kelly was amazed. 'Have you let the hospital know?'

'Oh yes.'

'And Ian?'

Laura giggled. 'No. Not yet. He would only have panicked, and there's hours to go yet.'

'You don't know that!' Kelly stood up, doing some panicking of her own. 'You have to get there as soon as possible.'

'But you promised we could tidy up first!'

'Jordan and I can do that when you've gone,' Kelly hustled her out of the room. 'I just hope you're poor husband doesn't faint with the shock of it.'

'So do—Ooh!' Laura gasped again, biting her lip. 'I think you're right, maybe I should get straight to the hospital.'

'I don't think it, I know it. You shouldn't have left it this long.'

Ian and Jordan were talking together when the two women entered the room, although Jordan immediately stopped the conversation and came over to Kelly.

'Are you all right?' His voice was huskily soft.

Any other time she might have questioned his concern for her, but right now she had more important things on her mind. 'It's Laura we have to be concerned about now,' she told him briskly. 'Ian, get the car out. Jordan, get Laura's case down from the bedroom.' Amazingly both women had forgotten it!

Ian gasped, paling. 'You mean—Laura, are you——'

'Of course she is,' Kelly said impatiently. 'Now will you bring the car round?'

'I'll drive them,' Jordan put in quietly. 'I don't think Ian is in any condition to drive anywhere.'

'A good idea,' she agreed with him. Ian seemed to have gone to pieces, asking Laura repeatedly how she felt, and not seeming to believe her when she assured him she felt fine. 'And I think it should be now.'

'What about you?'

'Laura wants the dining-room tidied. I don't think she'll go if I don't promise to do it.'

'I don't like leaving you.' His gaze was intent on her still pale face. 'Not when you aren't feeling well yourself.'

'I'm all right now. Really,' she insisted as he went to protest. 'Just get her to the hospital.'

She finally managed to get them out of the house, Ian sitting in the back of the car with Laura while Jordan drove them. 'And I want to know the minute the baby is born,' she instructed.

'You take care of yourself,' Laura ordered meaningly. 'We'll send Jordan straight back to you.'

'Thank you,' he put in dryly. 'I thought I asked you not to make it tonight,' he teased.

Laura giggled, some of the tension easing. 'I could make it right here in your car if you don't hurry!'

'Heaven forbid!' Jordan groaned, putting the car into gear. 'I'll be back soon, Kelly.'

She stood and watched them until the tail-lights of the car disappeared in the distance, going back into the house to methodically wash and dry up before tidying the kitchen as well as the dining-room, glad of something to do to take her mind off Laura and the coming baby.

Eight months from now she would be going through the same thing Laura was now experiencing—and Jordan wouldn't be there. It was curiously ironic that he should drive Laura to the hospital, when he wouldn't even know of his own child's birth.

Jordan arrived back just over an hour later, joining Kelly in the lounge. 'It could be hours yet,' he shrugged. 'Ian's promised to call us as soon as there's any news. Right now I intend getting you home to bed. You look washed out.'

Kelly flushed. 'I feel fine.'

'You don't look it,' he said firmly. 'Home, to bed and a hot drink.'

'And you?' she asked huskily, suddenly longing for his closeness.

'Me?' he echoed sharply, turning away. 'No,' he said tautly, 'I don't think so.'

She lapsed into silence, joining him in the warm interior of the car. She had needed him tonight, and once again he had rejected her. She wouldn't ever ask again.

Her father was already in bed when they got home, and yawning tiredly Kelly elected to go to her bedroom. Jordan made no effort to stop her, his mood once more taciturn and unapproachable.

She had been in bed several minutes when the light knock sounded on the door. Jordan entered at her surprised acknowledgement, a tray in his hand.

'Cocoa,' he said at her questioning look, sitting on the side of the bed.

She took the mug from him, the colour high in her

cheeks. She hadn't expected to see him again this evening, and his presence here now unnerved her. 'What's that?' she eyed the tablet he held out to her.

'You're over-excited, and this waiting to hear about Laura won't do you any good. This is just a sleeping tablet——'

'No!' she recoiled in horror. 'I don't want it!'

'It won't harm you. It's only one of the tablets prescribed to help your father sleep.'

And could do irrevocable harm to her baby! 'I don't like taking drugs of any kind,' she said stiffly.

'Neither do I. But this isn't taking drugs for the sake of it. I just happen to believe you need to sleep right now.'

Kelly knew of a much more pleasurable way of helping her sleep, and her cheeks became flushed at her thoughts. She knew Jordan had guessed them by the sharpening of his gaze, and she bristled angrily. 'I'll get to sleep without the use of drugs,' she told him tautly, and turned on to her side, her back towards him. 'Goodnight,' her voice was muffled.

She could hear him moving about the room, and suddenly felt the other side of the bed give as he climbed in beside her, the warmth of his naked body curved into the back of hers. She had stiffened at the first touch of his flesh against her, but as usual the warm tide of sensuality washed over her, trembling as he caressed the curve of her waist and thigh.

'Turn out the light,' he murmured against her earlobe, biting gently into her skin.

'Jordan . . .' she said achingly.

'Don't turn me away, Kelly. Not tonight. I need you.'

She had no intention of turning him away, reaching out her hand to turn off the light before rolling over to face him. What followed was beautiful, the complete opposite of their last two intimate encounters. Jordan made wild, beautiful love to her, raising her to the heights and holding her there until he took them both trembling over the edge to ecstatic delight.

Jordan had already left the bedroom when she woke the next morning, but she had a memory of them closely entwined all night. As usual no word had been spoken between them, and yet the wonder still stayed with Kelly, the warmth and love she felt towards Jordan threatening to overwhelm her.

If only it could always be this way! But it couldn't. Soon her pregnancy would be obvious even to the least discerning eye—and Jordan was far from being that! He saw all too much.

He came into the room now without knocking, carrying a breakfast tray this time. 'Laura tells me I'm to give breakfast in bed to her son's godmother,' he explained with a smile.

Kelly's eyes lit up with pleasure and she sat up in the bed, pulling the sheet up to cover her nakedness as Jordan's gaze unashamedly lingered on her bare breasts. 'Laura has a son?' she asked excitedly.

'Ian does too,' he told her mockingly.

She gave him an impatient glance. 'How are they both?'

'Well, Ian is bearing up very well. All right, all right!' he held his hands up defensively as Kelly looked like throwing a pillow at him. 'Laura and the baby are both doing well. He weighed seven pounds six ounces, and has been named Anthony Michael.'

'After Laura's father,' Kelly nodded.

'And Ian's,' Jordan put in dryly.

Kelly eyed him mischievously. 'Are you going to stand there all day with my breakfast?'

With a smile he placed the tray across her legs. 'I seem

to remember you only liked tea and toast for your breakfast.'

'Lovely,' she smiled up at him. 'Am I really going to be
Anthony's godmother?'

'Mm.' He sat on the bed beside her, very dark and
virile in faded denims and blue fitted shirt. 'And I'm de-
signated the role of godfather,' he drawled.

Kelly busied herself with buttering her toast and pour-
ing out her tea. 'And when do they expect the christening
to take place?' she asked casually.

'I don't suppose they've really thought about it. When
do they usually take place?'

'About six months after the birth, I think.'

'Then that's when they'll have it.'

'But we won't be together then,' she reminded him.

'No,' Jordan said tightly, 'I don't suppose we will.'

'You know we won't.' Kelly sipped her tea, feeling the
nausea leaving her.

'Last night meant—nothing to you?' He stood up,
moving to look out of the window.

Kelly looked up at him, wishing she could read
something of his mood from the broadness of his back and
muscular shoulders. 'Did it mean anything to you?'

He spun round, pinpointing her with his icy grey eyes.
'I asked first.'

She looked down at her toast. 'It—I enjoyed it,' she
admitted frankly.

She could feel his violence reaching out to her across
the room. 'I know that, damn you!' he snapped savagely.
'I asked if it *meant* anything?'

Kelly's expression was challenging. 'And I asked you
the same thing.'

'Oh, to hell with it!' He slammed out of the room.

Her father had just finished his breakfast when she came
down the stairs, looking up to smile at her. 'What's going

on?' he asked her. 'First of all Jordan says he's taking the day off work and now he's gone in after all.'

That was news to Kelly, both the day off and the fact that Jordan had now gone to work. 'He's busy,' she shrugged off the subject. 'Where did you get to last night?' she asked him teasingly.

'Didn't Jordan tell you?' He went slightly red.

'No.' Kelly noticed the high flush to his cheeks. 'Come on, Dad, tell me about it. You look like a pleased little boy.'

He blushed again. 'I think I'm in love, Kelly,' he told her almost ruefully.

'Dad!' Her eyes widened. 'When did this happen?'

'The last few weeks,' he said bashfully.

'And am I allowed to know the name of this woman you love?'

'You already know her,' he smiled. 'I'm in love with Anne—Anne Fellows.'

'Anne——?' Kelly paled. 'I—I didn't realise.'

Oh God, her father had fallen in love with the woman who was secretly meeting Jordan! It seemed that both she and her father had been taken for a fool. But how could Jordan let her father be used like that? Even though he had no love for her she had at least thought Jordan liked and respected her father.

'Well, I'm a bit old to be thinking of marrying again,' her father began.

'At fifty-one?' she teased, feeling numb inside.

'Even at forty-six,' he grimaced. 'But I am seriously thinking about it. How would you feel about having Anne as your stepmother?'

Kelly bit her lip. 'Don't you think you should ask her first?'

'I suppose so. I hear your friend had her baby,' he changed the subject.

'Mm. I thought I'd telephone the hospital and see if I

could get in to see her today.' She had been going to ask Jordan to go with her, and wanted to test his reaction to the baby, but now that was out of the question. 'I think I'll give them a call now.'

'Are you sure going to the hospital is a good idea?' her father asked in a worried voice.

Kelly gave him a sharp glance. 'What do you mean?'

He looked uncomfortable now. 'I—You—Jordan told me about your losing the baby five years ago,' he explained awkwardly.

'Oh, did he?' she said dully. She shrugged. 'I'm over that now, Daddy.' Besides, she had a new life growing inside her, a life that just *had* to flourish. Nothing would happen to this baby, she wouldn't let it. 'And Laura would think if odd if I didn't go.'

'I suppose so,' he agreed reluctantly.

Kelly visited Laura several times during the next week, loving little Anthony Michael. He was a very contented baby, lying quite happily in his crib, unless of course he wanted his food. Jordan visited Laura too, although at different times from Kelly; he also sent a lovely bouquet of white roses, and a huge teddy bear for Anthony.

'It's bigger than he is,' Laura joked once she was back in her own home again, the baby asleep upstairs in his nursery.

'He'll grow,' Kelly smiled.

Laura had been home two days now, and it was ten days since the baby's birth, ten days during which Kelly hardly ever saw Jordan. If he wasn't working then he was out, on business or simply for his own pleasure he didn't bother to tell her. In fact, they hardly spoke any more, not since the morning Jordan had slammed out of her bedroom.

'And you,' Laura said gently, interrupting her thoughts. 'You're growing nicely, too.'

Kelly looked down ruefully at her thickening waistline. 'Aren't I just?' she grimaced.

'Jordan still doesn't know?'

She looked away. 'No.'

'And the doctor, have you seen him yet?'

'This afternoon.'

'Well, at least that's something,' Laura said approvingly.

'I've been putting it off,' she admitted. 'I'm not greatly enamoured of doctors myself. But Paul Anderson is very good.'

Laura nodded. 'I've heard that he is.'

Kelly stood up. 'I have to be going now, my appointment is in half an hour.'

'I hope everything goes all right,' Laura told her. 'You'll call me?'

Kelly assured her she would. 'Don't get up,' she advised as Laura tried to struggled to her feet, bending down to kiss her affectionately on the cheek. Laura and she had become very close the last few weeks, and Laura was the nearest thing she had to a sister.

Kelly waited nervously outside the doctor's office, the receptionist occasionally giving her a friendly smile. She knew her pregnancy was a reality, that wasn't what was worrying her. She just had a dread of being told there was anything wrong with this pregnancy.

She looked up as Paul Anderson came out of his office, a welcoming smile on his face. He was a tall loose-limbed man in his early fifties, still quite handsome, although his hair was iron grey now.

'Mrs Lord,' he shook her hand warmly as she stood up. 'Come into my office,' he invited, seeing her seated before going behind the mahogany desk and sitting opposite her. 'I was hoping to see you here again,' he smiled.

Kelly played with the strap of her handbag, her hands suddenly hot and clammy. She sat on the edge of her seat, every muscle poised for flight. 'You—you were?' she licked her lips nervously.

'Oh yes,' he nodded. 'Your husband isn't with you?'

'Er—no. He—he had to work.'

'Mm, I remember he was a busy man. Still, shall we get the examination over with first, and then we can discuss things more clearly.'

Kelly suffered the examination with gritted teeth, although Paul Anderson couldn't have been gentler, and dressed with shaking hands while he went to wash his hands.

'Well,' he gave a satisfied smile 'I'm happy to diagnose that you are pregnant.'

Her breath left her in a sigh, relieved it had been confirmed, even if she had already known it to be fact.

He wrote something down in his notes, Kelly's file open in front of him. 'Five or six weeks, I should say,' he murmured thoughtfully.

'Six and a half,' Kelly muttered.

His raised questioning blue eyes. 'You're that sure of the date?'

Her cheeks blazed with colour. 'Yes.'

'Oh well, that stops a lot of speculation. Of course, the same problems are going to apply.'

She frowned her puzzlement. 'Problems?'

'Yes,' he smiled. 'You're going to have to be just as careful.'

'But surely that's only natural?'

'I meant extra-careful, as you were before.'

'Not careful enough, apparently,' she recalled with some bitterness.

'No,' the doctor agreed gravely. 'Perhaps this time you'll remember that pregnant ladies, especially ones as delicate as you, do not go running about the streets,' he told her sternly.

Kelly looked even more puzzled. 'Delicate? *I'm* delicate?'

'Extremely so,' he nodded.

She licked her lips. 'Tell me more.'

He shrugged. 'It's the same as before, nothing has changed. You have a weakness to your muscles that makes it extremely difficult for you to carry a child the full nine months. Your husband will have told you——'

'Jordan?' she cut in sharply, hardly able to believe what he was telling her.

'Yes—Jordan. I'm sure he doesn't relish being banished from your bed once again,' he gave a sympathetic smile. 'Although this time you'll have the advantage of not being newlyweds.'

Kelly was very pale, finding it more and more difficult to take in what the doctor was telling her. 'Are you saying that you advised Jordan to sleep in a separate bedroom to me five years ago?'

'Not exactly. But under the circumstances I'm sure he would have found it difficult sharing a bed with you and not being able to continue a normal relationship.'

'My God!' she gasped. All this time she had thought Jordan had been disgusted by her pregnancy, and in reality he had merely been protecting her and their unborn child. Oh heavens, what did it all mean?

CHAPTER TEN

WHEN she came to she was lying on top of the black leather couch in the doctor's surgery, and Paul Anderson was anxiously waiting for her to wake up. It all came back to her now—her difficulty in carrying a child, Jordan's protectiveness in the past. But why hadn't he told her, explained why he had left her alone in their bed night after night?

'You didn't know, did you?' the doctor sighed.

'No,' she said shakily, 'I—I had no idea.'

'I naturally assumed that your husband would have told you by now.'

'My husband and I separated just after I lost the baby,' she told him dully, swinging her legs to the floor and sitting up.

'I see.' He looked slightly taken aback. 'Then this baby——'

'Is his,' Kelly interrupted firmly. 'A temporary reconciliation,' she blushed at his questioning look. 'But that isn't important now, what is important, to me at least, is that I don't lose this baby.'

'It's important to me too, Mrs Lord,' Paul Anderson told her gravely.

'Of course it is—I'm sorry. I didn't mean to appear rude.' She was just so shocked by what he had told her that she couldn't even think straight! 'Just tell me what I have to do to keep this baby and I'll to it. Anything,' she stressed vehemently.

'Well . . .'

'Yes?' she demanded to know. 'Do you have

something in mind?'

He nodded. 'But it isn't very pleasant.'

'I said anything, Dr Anderson, and that's exactly what I meant.'

'All right,' he shrugged. 'But don't say I didn't warn you. The ideal solution is for you to spend the duration of your pregnancy in bed, either at home or in a nursing home.'

'All of it?' she asked incredulously.

'I'm afraid so. That way there would be hardly any risk.'

'Then I'll do it,' Kelly decided. 'When would it have to start?'

'As soon as possible.' The doctor frowned. 'You're sure about this? It isn't a decision to be made lightly. Perhaps you should discuss it with your husband first.'

'No,' she looked down at her hands. 'I told you, our reconciliation was temporary.' She lifted her head proudly. 'It's over.' She now knew the reason Jordan had moved out of their bedroom, but that in no way excused his affair with Angela Divine. Most men wouldn't have found it too difficult to remain faithful to a delicately pregnant wife, but with Jordan's high sex drive he hadn't been able to remain faithful for even a matter of weeks, let alone months.

'I see,' he said thoughtfully, obviously not 'seeing' at all.

'I'll want to go into a nursing home,' she told him briskly. 'Perhaps you could recommend one?'

'I could . . .'

'Then do so,' she encouraged.

'Very well,' he accepted with a shrug, 'I could arrange it all for you from here if you would prefer it?'

'Yes, perhaps that might be more suitable.' She stood up in conclusion of the meeting. 'I'll telephone later today and confirm any arrangements you may have made.'

'Maybe it would be better if I called you——'

'No! No,' she repeated more calmly. 'I may not be there, and I—I want to take the call myself. You're my doctor, and as you're my doctor all of this meeting today is privileged information?'

'Yes,' he acknowledged slowly.

'And if someone were to ask about me, anything at all, you wouldn't tell them?'

'Not if I were asked not to.'

'Then I'm asking you,' Kelly said calmly.

'Does this request include the husband you're now parted from?' he guessed shrewdly.

'Especially him,' she confirmed shakily.

'Are you sure that's wise?' the doctor asked gently. 'Surely this is exactly the time you're going to need him the most?'

'Our marriage is over,' she insisted. 'I'll telephone you later today, Dr Anderson.'

She left his office in a daze. She needed someone to talk to, someone who knew the whole story about the past and would understand. Only one person presented herself— Maggie.

Her friend looked surprised to see her when she rang the doorbell a few minutes later. 'Hello, stranger.' She opened the door further for Kelly to enter. 'What brings you here?'

Kelly burst into tears, deep racking sobs that shook her slender body. 'Oh, Maggie!' she cried, burying her face in her friend's shoulder.

'Hey!' the other girl chided. 'I didn't mean you weren't welcome.'

'I know,' Kelly sniffed, gradually growing calmer.

'What's happened?' Maggie smoothed Kelly's dark hair, drying her tears with a tissue. 'Has that brute been bullying you again?'

'You mean Jordan?' she gave a watery smile.

'Well, what other bully do we both know?' Maggie said dryly.

'He isn't a brute,' Kelly sniffed again, taking the tissue and blowing her nose. 'He can be quite gentle at times.'

'I don't——' Maggie broke off as the flat door was opened by someone with a key. A man entered the room, very casually dressed in denims and a tee-shirt, his fair hair long and untidy. 'What are you doing here?' Maggie demanded of him.

'I forgot my notebook.' He reached across the desk in the corner of the room, picking up the pad. 'Aren't you going to introduce us?' he eyed Kelly pointedly.

Kelly supposed this must be the boy-friend, although he wasn't exactly what she had been expecting. She had somehow imagined him to be suave and sophisticated. Not that he wasn't good-looking, he was, just not what Kelly had thought he would be.

She looked at Maggie questioningly. It wasn't like her to forget her manners in this way. 'I'm Kelly Lord,' she introduced herself when it appeared Maggie had been struck dumb.

His eyes widened. '*The* Kelly Lord?'

She shrugged. 'It depends what you mean by that.'

'Wife of Jordan Lord,' he drawled. 'Daughter of David Darrow.'

'That's me,' she nodded. 'Should I know you, Mr——?'

'Ben!' Maggie said warningly.

'Okay, darling,' he grinned. 'No need to panic, I'm going now. Nice meeting you, Mrs Lord.' He nodded before leaving.

'Now what were we talking about?' Maggie said brittlely. 'Ah yes, Jordan. Now——'

'Maggie,' Kelly interrupted tautly, 'your boy-friend's name was Ben. It—It wouldn't be Ben Durston, would it?'

'Kelly——'

'Would it?' she demanded shrilly, a terrible feeling of inevitability washing over her.

'Yes,' Maggie admitted with some reluctance.

'The Ben Durston who wrote that story about my father?'

'Yes,' she sighed.

'It was you all the time!' Kelly accused. 'All this time we've been puzzling over it, and it was you. Why, Maggie?' she choked. 'Why did you do that to me?'

Maggie's eyes flashed angrily. 'I did it to keep Ben,' she snapped.

'But you said you were the one who was unsure of your relationship, not him,' she frowned.

'So I lied.'

'And you betrayed a confidence to keep him,' Kelly said disgustedly.

'I'd do anything to keep him,' Maggie told her vehemently.

'I thought we were friends!'

'We are, but when it comes to men it's another matter. Ask Jordan about that,' Maggie's mouth twisted. 'I'm sure he would be only too pleased to tell you about the times I tried to get him into bed with me.'

Kelly went deathly white. 'What are you saying? You and Jordan . . .?'

'No,' she gave a harsh laugh. '*Not* me and Jordan. Although it wasn't for want of trying on my part.'

'Jordan turned you down?'

'Oh yes,' she confirmed angrily. 'The bastard! Even after you'd left him he still didn't want to know.'

'He said you had been to see him,' Kelly remembered dully.

'One last try,' Maggie nodded. 'He was just as insulting as ever. God, how I hate him—still want him too,' she revealed bitterly.

'And that's why Jordan doesn't like or trust you.' Kelly spoke almost to herself. It also explained his comparison to Judas. Jordan must have known all along exactly what sort of friend Maggie was to her.

Maggie shrugged. 'Now I suppose you feel the same way.'

'Yes,' she agreed unhesitantly. 'You have no morals or principles.'

'And we both know you do,' Maggie scorned. 'It didn't help you keep your precious Jordan, though, did it?'

'You disgust me!' Kelly told her before leaving.

So much for her avoiding all upsets and excitement during her pregnancy! So far she had been told just how delicate she really was, had found out that Maggie's boyfriend was the reporter Ben Durston, and now it appeared Maggie had been chasing Jordan for years. It was all so hard to take in.

She was still in a daze when she arrived home, blinking as Mrs McLeod hurried across the hallway in a harassed manner. 'Is there anything wrong?' Kelly asked her.

'Nothing at all,' the housekeeper beamed at her. 'Everything is wonderful. You see——'

'That's all right, Mrs McLeod.' Jordan had appeared as if from nowhere. 'Take the champagne through to Mr Darrow when you have it, and tell him that Mrs Lord and I will join him in a moment.'

Kelly watched as the woman hurried in the direction of the kitchen, feeling her arm taken in a firm grasp as Jordan took her into his study. She looked at him nervously, wondering about the champagne. Surely Dr Anderson hadn't broken his promise to her?

'Your father and Anne have just announced their engagement,' Jordan put her mind at rest about knowing of the baby.

For a moment what he had said didn't hit her, then

she gave a disbelieving laugh. 'Oh no, Jordan, now that I just won't allow.'

His eyes narrowed. '*You* won't allow it?' His voice was deceptively soft.

'No, I won't.' She gave a firm shake of her head. 'You may have affairs with whom you please, but you will not involve my father in it.'

'Affair . . .? Are you implying that I've been having an affair with Anne?' he demanded tautly.

Kelly was unmoved by his anger; the child inside her gave her a confidence that might otherwise have been lacking. 'I'm more than implying it, Jordan. You see, I saw you together at a restaurant a few weeks ago.'

'You saw *me* with Anne?' He sounded incredulous.

'Yes.'

'But I—I know! Yes, I was with her—but so was your father,' he announced grimly.

'You were alone!'

'Your father arrived later than we did. If you'd stayed around a little longer to *spy* on me you would probably have seen him join us.'

Kelly still eyed him suspiciously. 'Just supposing that's true——'

'It is,' he snapped.

'If it's true why were you all so secretive about it?'

Jordan lips clamped together, and he seemed to be in deep thought. 'You intend leaving me anyway, don't you?' he said finally.

'As soon as possible,' she confirmed.

'Then I have nothing to lose,' he shrugged resignedly. 'Your father regained his memory that day. If you remember he was heavily sedated when you arrived home?'

Only one thing seemed important to her at the moment. 'My father has his memory back?' she repeated dazedly. 'He remembers everything?'

'Yes,' Jordan admitted heavily.

Her last worry was removed. She had been debating how she could suddenly disappear when her father was still ill, now that obstacle had been taken away she could leave with a clear conscience. There just remained the puzzle of why she hadn't been told of his recovery weeks ago.

'Why do you think?' Jordan answered her query as to why.

She shook her head, too weary to think. 'I have no idea.'

'You surprise me,' he drawled. 'Just lately you seem to be the one with all the answers.'

'I have one now too,' she told him dully. 'Ben Durston is Maggie's live-in boy-friend.'

He whistled through his teeth. 'I shouldn't be surprised, but somehow it just didn't occur to me. Other things on my mind, I suppose,' he said ruefully.

'Such as?' Kelly asked softly.

Jordan sighed. 'You, mainly!

'Jordan,' she bit her lip, 'Maggie told me how she'd been after you for years, I—I just want to say I'm sorry I misjudged you concerning her. She really wasn't a true friend.' Her mouth trembled with emotion. 'In fact, she's been anything but that. Why didn't you tell me about her?'

'And ruin all your illusions about her?' he mocked, shaking his head. 'I couldn't do that to you.'

'And yet you've hurt me in so many other ways.'

'I haven't mean to,' he denied huskily.

'Having an affair with Angela Divine wasn't supposed to hurt me?' Kelly scorned.

He frowned darkly, sighing his impatience. 'Do you think I have affairs with every woman I meet?'

'I know about that one.'

'The same way you *knew* about Anne and myself?'

She blushed at his intended rebuke. 'I heard you, you and Angela, discussing going away together.'

He looked stunned. 'I don't know what you're talking about,' he dismissed tersely. 'I didn't have an affair with Angela, and I certainly never discussed going away with her—unless it was on business?'

'Definitely not.'

Jordan shrugged. 'Then you're mistaken.'

'But I can't be! I heard you.'

'Tell me,' he invited softly.

She did so, leaving out none of her anger and frustration. She had to give him credit for nerve, he didn't look in the least perturbed by her disclosure.

'It was Ian,' he said at the end of her explanation.

Kelly looked puzzled. 'What was?'

'Ian was the one going away with Angie. Laura was the possessive woman in his life, and her father was the man with influence.'

She held her breath, horror in her eyes. 'No . . .' And yet hadn't Laura herself told her that Ian had been two-timing her at one time?

'Yes!' Jordan insisted savagely.

'Then all this time . . .'

'Yes, what about all this time, Kelly?' He moved forward to link his hands at the base of her spine. 'Just when did you hear this little conversation?'

It was too much, too many shocks in one day. She leant her head wearily against Jordan's chest. 'It was——' she closed her eyes to shut out the pain. 'It was the day I lost the baby,' she revealed in a rush.

She heard his ragged intake of breath, and his arms pressed painfully into her sides. 'Did it happen—because of that?' he asked shakily.

'Yes. Oh *God*, yes!'

'You little fool!' he groaned, gathering her close, his

face buried in her hair. 'Don't you realise that you could have died too?'

She looked up at him with tear-stained cheeks. 'I could?'

'You aren't strong enough to have children,' he muttered into her hair.

'Is that why you moved out of our bedroom?' She stroked the thick dark hair at his nape, wanting his version of what had happened. 'Why you left me when I needed you beside me?'

He was trembling against her—strong, forceful Jordan trembling! 'And do you think I didn't need you?' he sounded agonised. 'But I couldn't be near you and not want to make love to you. I had to let you sleep alone because I couldn't keep my hands off you. I still can't.'

'Jordan . . .?' She held her breath, almost afraid to hope.

'I love you, Kelly,' he groaned. 'Surely you've realised that by now?'

She blinked back the tears, tears of happiness. 'Love, Jordan?' she choked.

'Yes—*love*! Insanely, passionately, mindlessly. I've always loved you, right from the moment I first saw you. I would have married you immediately, but your father insisted I wait. You see, I'm what could be called a freak, emotionally. I have a quirk in my nature that isn't very pleasant. Your father recognised it and was worried for you. With just cause,' he added grimly.

'But what is it?' Kelly searched his face worriedly. 'What's wrong with you?' she demanded to know.

Jordan swung away from her, his shoulders hunched. 'I have a disease, a sickness,' he said abruptly. 'It's eating me up alive.'

'Jordan!' she cried. 'Tell me what's wrong with you!'

'I'm obsessed with you!' He turned to her with tortured eyes. 'If I could lock you away from other people, allow no one else to see you, I would. I'm jealous of anyone who so much as looks at you, talks to you. When I thought the baby might take you away from me I went completely to pieces. It could have killed you, taken you away from me for good. If you'd died I think I would have killed myself.'

'But—but you let me go.'

'Yes,' he sighed. 'I let you go before I destroyed you.'

'It was thinking you didn't love me that was destroying me.'

'Not love you?' he scorned derisively. 'Sometimes I wish to God I didn't. This obsession with you is completely against my nature. Until you came into my life I lived perfectly normally, I had my women friends and they meant nothing to me. As soon as you walked into the room I began to vibrate with this burning obsession, and it hasn't stopped for a moment since. When you walked out on me I used to lie awake every night plotting ways of getting you back, but by morning I would have come to my senses. I'm no good for you, Kelly. And you make me weak where usually I'm strong.'

'And how would you feel about my marrying someone else?' she asked softly.

His eyes seemed to burn, his expression dangerous. 'I'll never let you belong to another man! I'd kill you first.' He shook with a rage that made his breathing ragged, his fists clenched.

'But I want children, Jordan. At least two. I want——'

'You still want children, even though you know it could kill you?'

She nodded. 'It's important to me.'

'And you're important to me.' He pulled her roughly

against him. 'God, I can't go on without you any more, Kelly. Don't leave me again,' he pleaded. 'Stay with me. Be my wife again.'

'And children?'

'Never!' he said forcefully. 'I won't see you exposed to that danger again. I couldn't bear the torture for nine months, each day wondering if I'm going to lose you. It drove me to drink last time.'

She knew, oh God, how she knew. She had never guessed that Jordan kept all this molten emotion inside him. Maybe he had been wise to keep it from her five years ago, to encase this fierce love behind a wall of cool mockery. Five years ago she would have been terrified by the intensity of his love for her, now she would have revelled in it. But it was too late, too late. Jordan couldn't go through the agony of this pregnancy with her, it could just kill him.

She pulled out of his arms. 'I can't come back to you, Jordan.' She sounded much calmer than she felt.

His hands dropped to his sides, a look of utter defeat on his face. 'I knew this obsession would frighten the hell out of you. It would frighten any woman.' Suddenly his gaze was sharp. 'Or is it just that you no longer love me? You used to love me, used to tell me all the time, and I daren't even tell you back in case I went berserk and made an absolute fool of myself.'

Poor Jordan, how he had suffered for loving her so much. Her father's referrence to Jordan not being an easy man to live with now made sense; he had known of the strength, the singlemindedness of Jordan's love, and had been concerned for her.

'I wouldn't have minded,' she told him huskily.

He looked at her with pained grey eyes. 'And now it's too late?'

'Much too late. Maybe one day——'

'Don't make promises you can't keep,' he rasped harshly. 'Our marriage is finally at an end.'

'Don't say that,' she choked. 'Just give me time.' Seven months!

'After five years I think you know whether or not you can live with me. It's all right, Kelly, I understand. I couldn't live with this possessiveness either, it would make me claustrophobic. You know the truth about your father now, so I'll leave as soon as I've drunk a toast to his future happiness,' he said bitterly.

Kelly frowned. 'Why was the truth kept from me? Why not tell me my father had regained his memory?' He still hadn't answered that question—although he had answered a lot of others!

'Because I wanted another chance with you.' He shrugged. 'It couldn't work, not living with you like this. I only have to look at you to shake with wanting you. Sharing a bedroom with you was purgatory. I couldn't be with you and not make love with you.'

'But my father——'

'Believed you had always loved me, even when we were apart. He thought I should have this chance too. He wanted you to be happy, and he thought I could achieve that. He was wrong, and so was I. You can stay here, I'll be moving out.'

'That won't be necessary,' she assured him hastily. 'I—I intend going away for a while. I thought I might go on a cruise or something, travel.'

Jordan frowned. 'Your father won't like that.'

'I'm not asking anyone if I can go, Jordan,' she told him in a controlled voice, making herself sound cool and assured.

His mouth twisted. 'Certainly not me.'

'No,' she agreed huskily.

'Okay.' He braced his shoulders, as if recovering from a

blow. 'Let's go and put on a show for your father and Anne.'

'Jordan . . .' her voice broke, 'I'm really sorry.'

'So am I,' he said heavily.

Please, let this time go quickly, she prayed silently.

It didn't, it dragged. And yet in the end it was all worth it. Nothing went wrong this time, and when the time came for the birth it all went off quite normally.

During Kelly's months in the nursing home her only visitor had been Laura, sworn to secrecy, even from Ian this time. And she had telephoned her father constantly, reassuring all his anxieties as to her whereabouts. His own newly married status had taken the pressure off her somewhat, although he never ceased asking when she was coming home from her travels.

Jordan had remained at the house this time, and according to her father he was working harder than ever, suicidally so. Well, his suffering was now at an end; she could leave hospital. She took a taxi straight to the house, the carrycot on the backseat beside her.

Mrs McLeod looked taken aback when she opened the door. 'Mrs Lord . . .' she took in the suitcase standing at Kelly's feet at a glance. 'Are you back to stay?' she asked excitedly, her pleasure evident.

'I am,' Kelly grinned. 'But I'm not alone.'

Mrs McLeod looked behind Kelly at the apparently empty taxi. She frowned her puzzlement.

Kelly laughed. 'Come and help me,' she invited.

The housekeeper followed her in a daze. 'I don't understand . . .'

'You will,' Kelly promised.

'Let me do that, love,' the driver insisted as he saw her intention of getting the carrycot out of the back. 'You shouldn't be lifting yet.'

'Thank you,' she accepted gratefully. 'Although I'm quite well.'

'My wife has had three,' he told her as he took the carrycot into the lounge, 'so I'm sure you still tire very easily.'

Kelly gave him a generous tip for his kindness, then turned to find a stunned Mrs McLeod peering into the carrycot.

'I—You—I——'

'It's all right,' Kelly laughed. 'I know just how you feel.'

The housekeeper stared to beam. 'I'm sure you don't.'

'But I do,' she insisted happily. 'How do you feel about baby-sitting for half an hour? I'm just going to the office to bring Jordan home to lunch.'

'I'd love to baby-sit,' Mrs McLeod said eagerly. 'Mr Lord's going to be so pleased to see you.'

'I hope so. I really hope so.'

'He will be. But I'm afraid this,' Kelly indicated the carrycot, 'is going to come as something of a surprise to him.'

'A pleasant one, I hope. Make it a celebration lunch, Mrs McLeod,' she stooped to kiss her sleeping offspring. 'Feeding time isn't for another two hours, so you should be all right.'

The housekeeper was looking disappointed. 'And I was hoping to get a little cuddle.'

'Don't worry,' she laughed. 'You'll have plenty of time for that.'

'Oh, Mrs Lord . . .' Mrs McLeod said tearfully.

'I know,' Kelly squeezed her hand. 'Now, half an hour,' she warned before leaving the house.

Janet looked as surprised to see her as Mrs McLeod had been, although she recovered her equilibrium very well. 'I'll tell Mr Lord you're here,' she said politely.

'No, don't do that,' Kelly stopped her from buzzing Jordan's office. 'I want to surprise him,' she explained.

Janet raised her eyebrows. 'Oh, I think you'll do that.'

'My husband will be out to lunch,' Kelly told the other girl. 'And could you cancel his appointments for the rest of the day. And don't put any calls through.'

'I'm not sure——'

'Cancel them, Janet,' Kelly told her firmly before letting herself into Jordan's office.

He looked up as soon as she entered the room, obviously not used to people walking in on him in this way. He looked ill, very gaunt and pale, his hair even greyer at the temples. There was a look of bleak unhappiness about him, and Kelly knew she was the cause of it. She hoped she would be the one to dispel it too.

'Kelly . . .' He stood up slowly, a quickfire emotion flickering into his eyes.

She was heartened by that emotion, believing it to be the love he had hidden from her for so long, a love she now felt able to accept to the full. 'Hello, darling,' she greeted him huskily.

He swallowed hard. 'Darling . . .?' he repeated dazedly.

'Yes—darling.' She instantly went to him, putting her arms about his waist below his jacket, her head resting on his chest, the fast beat of his heart sounding like a drum. 'I've missed you so,' she told him shakily.

His arms closed fiercely about her. 'God knows I've missed you too,' he groaned, his face buried in her throat. 'Where have you been?' he demanded to know, holding her at arms' length. 'I've had people looking for you everywhere!'

'You have?' Her eyes widened.

'Of course. You can't just disappear like that without worrying me out of my mind.'

'But I telephoned my father.'

'That isn't the same,' Jordan rasped. 'Where have you been, Kelly?'

'I'll tell you later.'

'You'll tell me now.'

'No, I won't. Right now we're going home to lunch.'

'Home? Our home?' he asked incredulously.

'Yes.' She took his hand, leading him towards the door. 'Mrs McLeod will have everything ready for us.'

He stopped dead. 'What is this, Kelly? Another go at trying to live with me? Because I don't need that. I can't go through losing you all again——' His voice broke emotionally.

'You aren't going to lose me. Jordan, I love you. I've always loved you. I never stopped for one moment, not even when I thought I hated you.'

He shook his head. 'But you left me.'

'And I had a good reason for that. I'll explain when we get home.'

'It had better be good,' he warned tautly.

'It is.' She took his hand again, smiling up at him adoringly.

His eyes darkened almost to black. 'God, you're beautiful!' he groaned, bending his head to devour her lips with his own. He was shaking by the time he drew back, his breathing ragged. 'I love you,' he told her throatily.

'Let's go home,' she murmured.

'You're going to stay?'

'Oh yes,' she smiled.

'Then let's go.' His arm went protectively about her waist. 'I'll be out for the rest of the day,' he told Janet as they passed through the outer office.

She nodded. 'I've already cancelled your appointments.'

'I asked her to,' Kelly explained at his questioning look.

'Do you intend taking over my life?' Jordan asked her once they were in the car.

'Completely,' she told him happily. 'You're going to enjoy being with me so much you'll never want to leave my side.'

'I never want to do that anyway,' he said deeply.

'Oh, Jordan, I love you,' she said with a catch in her throat.

'I hope to God you do, because I won't let you go again.' His hands were tight on the steering-wheel.

'I'm going to prove it to you as soon as I'm able,' she promised throatily.

'When we get home?' he quirked one eyebrow hopefully.

Kelly shook her head regretfully. 'I have other plans for when we get home.'

He frowned. 'Lunch can wait.'

'I didn't mean lunch.'

'Then what——'

She reached out and touched his thigh. 'Wait and see.'

His sighed his impatience but didn't press the matter. Kelly just hoped he wasn't going to be too shocked. Maybe she should have telephoned and explained the situation to him, but she daren't do that at the time, and now it was too late to do more than present him with a fait accompli.

Everything was very quiet when they entered the house, no baby crying to warn Jordan of its existence. The reason for that soon became obvious, Mrs McLeod was cradling the baby in her arms, talking in a soft voice as it gazed blankly up at her.

'What the hell——!' Jordan had gone grey, frozen to the spot.

'It's all right, darling,' Kelly touched his arm. 'Come and meet your son.'

'My son . . .?'

'Yes.' Kelly took the baby from the housekeeper, his blue babygrow still far too large for him, and placed him gently into his father's arms.

'I'll go and check on the food.' Mrs McLeod tactfully left the room.

'Kelly——,' Jordan was having trouble articulating. 'I can't—This baby——'

'Your son,' she confirmed, looking at the thatch of dark hair so like Jordan's, the determined chin that reflected his stormy little nature, having already proved how powerful his lungs were. He was too like Jordan to be anything other than his child.

Jordan sat down before he fell down, holding the baby awkwardly in his strong arms. 'You must have been expecting him when you left me,' he finally said raggedly. 'Did you know?'

'Yes.' She bit her lip. 'Jordan, there's more.' She looked at him pleadingly.

'More?' he choked. 'What else could there be?'

'Don't be angry with me, Jordan. Please!'

'I'm not angry, I'm just dazed, incredulous.'

She took a deep breath. 'Then you're going to be even more so in a moment.' She bent over the carrycot and lifted out a second tiny shawl-wrapped baby.

'Twins!' Jordan gasped.

'Your daughter,' she nodded, taking off the shawl to reveal the pink babygrow-covered baby.

'My God!' He shook his head. 'All this and you never let me know!'

'Because I couldn't bear to see you suffer!' she told him desperately. 'I couldn't stand your pain, don't you see that?'

'And instead you went through all that alone. What a coward you must think me!' His face was harsh with self-loathing as he looked down at the baby in his arms.

'You aren't a coward!' Kelly cried. 'And I didn't go through so much. I've spent the last seven months in bed, and the birth was so easy. I've had a lovely time.' She could never tell him of the lonely days when she had longed for him with a fierce desperation.

'Don't lie to me.' He wasn't fooled for a moment. 'What are their names?' He looked at his children with a tenderness that lightened Kelly's heart.

'They don't have any yet,' she smiled her relief. It was going to be all right, she knew it was. She grinned. 'They were the only babies at the nursing home that didn't have names. I didn't think it fair to decide on something that important on my own.'

'Thank you,' he said deeply. 'Care to swap?' he quirked an eyebrow teasingly. 'I have an urgent desire to hold my daughter.'

Kelly's expression was impish as she handed him the little girl, another tiny replica of Jordan. 'Don't you think I'm clever?'

'Very clever,' he drawled.

'Actually, Jordan, I do have one name, if you wouldn't mind? I wanted to call our daughter Jordana.'

His expression was searching, obviously remembering the baby they had lost. 'If you're sure that's what you want,' he said uncertainly.

'Oh, I'm sure,' she gave him a glowing smile. 'I'll let you name our son.'

'I'll have to give it some serious thought. After all, the poor little devil's got to have it for a lifetime. I—Oh. Er—Kelly,' he gave her a sideways glance, 'I'm not sure, but I think . . .'

'Nappy change?' she giggled. 'I'll show you how.' She put the wide-eyed baby boy she was holding back into the carrycot.

'You'll do no such thing!' Jordan stood up, handing their daughter to her. 'At this size they terrify the life out of me. I'll play football with them when they're bigger.' He moved to the telephone.

'Who are you calling?' She deftly changed the baby's nappy.

'Your father. I take it he doesn't know he's a grand-father?'

'No, I thought you should be the first to know.'

'Are you feeding them yourself?' he asked huskily.

'Jealous?' she teased, realising that to tease him was the best way of dealing with his obsessive love.

'Insanely,' he chuckled. 'You've grown cheeky, young lady. When you're strong enough I'll give you a sound beating. But right now I'm going to telephone your father and tell him what a clever girl you are.'

'Jordan,' she bit her lip, 'I can't——'

'I know,' he kissed her briefly on the mouth. 'I just want to hold you, darling, kiss you, tell you how much I love you. I can wait for anything else.'

'I——' She was cut off by the hungry wail of their daughter, their son soon joining in the demand to be fed. 'I don't think our children can wait any longer for their lunch,' she said ruefully.

'They can wait two minutes. I want to watch,' he told her huskily.

'Jordan!' she blushed fiery red.

'I want to see,' he said. 'Oh, Kelly, I'm so sorry for what I've put you through, although I don't think I could have stood the agony of it all. God, what a coward I am!'

'Don't keep apologising.' She put her fingers over his

lips, trembling as he kissed her creamy skin. 'We're together now, that's all that matters.'

'If you say so.'

'I do.'

'I can't wait for later,' he said throatily.

'Neither can I,' she smiled, already imagining the
pleasure of being held in his arms all night, their love for
each other now confessed by both of them.

ALL ABOUT TWINS

Anyone who has seen twin toddlers playing together no doubt envies them just a little bit—for who among us, when we were children, did not imagine for ourselves a twin brother or sister as the perfect playmate and conspirator? But for twins, growing up with a mirror image is a normal state of affairs. As young children, they undoubtedly wonder where everyone else's identical mate is!

The birth of twins usually evokes feelings of wonderment in many people, and it's easy to see why. For this phenomenon is one of nature's greatest mysteries. Identical twins occur when a single ovum or egg in the womb splits into two very soon after fertilization, ultimately resulting in two fetuses. Why this occurs is not known, nor why it occurs only in human beings. Other mammals can have litters of two or more, but the offspring are never identical.

Perhaps because of the biological mystery surrounding identical twins, their birth has been treated by some cultures as a terrifying event, and by others as wonderful good luck, with the twins sometimes considered sacred. The Zulus of Africa permanently separate twins at birth, while the Dogons, another African people, center their entire society around twins, building monuments to them in the villages. And the Shuswap Indians of British Columbia believe that when a twin bathed in a lake or river, rain would fall.

Many famous twins have appeared in mythology. The Egyptians had twin gods, Osiris and Set. Twins Romulus and Remus built the city of Rome, and Amphion and Zethus built the Greek city of Thebes. But perhaps most famous of all are Castor and Pollux, who were fathered by Zeus (king of the ancient Greek gods) and became the two stars of the constellation of Gemini—the Twins.

Take these 4 best-selling novels FREE

Harlequin Presents...

Take these 4 best-selling novels FREE

That's right! FOUR first-rate Harlequin romance novels by four world renowned authors, FREE, as your introduction to the Harlequin Presents Subscription Plan. Be swept along by these FOUR exciting, poignant and sophisticated novels . . . . Travel to the Mediterranean island of Cyprus in **Anne Hampson**'s "Gates of Steel" . . . to Portugal for **Anne Mather**'s "Sweet Revenge" . . . to France and **Violet Winspear**'s "Devil in a Silver Room" . . . and the sprawling state of Texas for **Janet Dailey**'s "No Quarter Asked."

Join the millions of avid Harlequin readers all over the world who delight in the magic of a really exciting novel. EIGHT great NEW titles published EACH MONTH! Each month you will get to know exciting, interesting, true-to-life people . . . . You'll be swept to distant lands you've dreamed of visiting . . . . Intrigue, adventure, romance, and the destiny of many lives will thrill you through each Harlequin Presents novel.

Harlequin Presents...

The very finest in romantic fiction

Get all the latest books before they're sold out!

As a Harlequin subscriber you actually receive your personal copies of the latest Presents novels immediately after they come off the press, so you're sure of getting all 8 each month.

Cancel your subscription whenever you wish!

You don't have to buy any minimum number of books. Whenever you decide to stop your subscription just let us know and we'll cancel all further shipments.

Your FREE gift includes

Sweet Revenge by **Anne Mather**
Devil in a Silver Room by **Violet Winspear**
Gates of Steel by **Anne Hampson**
No Quarter Asked by **Janet Dailey**

FREE Gift Certificate
and subscription reservation

Mail this coupon today!

In the U.S.A.
1440 South Priest Drive
Tempe, AZ 85281

In Canada
649 Ontario Street
Stratford, Ontario N5A 6W2

Harlequin Reader Service:

Please send me my **4** Harlequin Presents books free. Also, reserve a subscription to the 8 new Harlequin Presents novels published each month. Each month I will receive 8 new Presents novels at the low price of $1.75 each [*Total — $14.00 a month*]. There are no shipping and handling or any other hidden charges. I am free to cancel at any time, but even if I do, these first 4 books are still mine to keep absolutely FREE without any obligation.

NAME   (PLEASE PRINT)

ADDRESS   (APT. NO.)

CITY   STATE / PROV.   ZIP / POSTAL CODE

Offer expires January 31, 1983
Offer not valid to present subscribers   SB518

If price changes are necessary, you will be notified.

NOW...

8 NEW

Harlequin  *Presents...*

EVERY MONTH!

Romance readers everywhere have expressed their delight with Harlequin Presents, along with their wish for more of these outstanding novels by world-famous romance authors. Harlequin is proud to meet this growing demand with 2 more NEW Presents every month—a total of 8 NEW Harlequin Presents every month!

MORE of the most popular romance fiction in the world!